Sometimes the Angels Weep

Sometimes the Angels Weep

Short Fiction

Michael Hiebert

DangerBoy Books
British Columbia, Canada

Published by DangerBoy Books Publishing, British Columbia, Canada.

ISBN-13: 978-1-927600-01-6
ISBN-10: 1-927600-01-4

DangerBoy Books Trade Paperback Edition.
First Printing, March 2013.
Printed in the United States of America.

All DangerBoy titles are available at special quantity discounts for bulk purchases for sales promotion, premiums, fund-raising, educational, or institutional use.

For Shannon,
who's waited much too long
for a book dedicated to her,
and spends far too much time
waiting for me in general.

Contents

Acknowledgments

I'd like to thank Annie Daylon for giving me the idea to put together this anthology. I am planning for another, humongous anthology to come down the pipe hopefully next year sometime, but she convinced me that I needed something now, even if it was smaller. And so, here it is. If you like what you're seeing, or enjoy what you read, you have her to thank (or blame, as the case may be). The other anthology is probably still coming; it's called *Fallen* and is at least double the size of the one you now hold in your hands.

Annie is a magnificent writer, and you can find her on the web at www.anniedaylon.com. She's also a voracious tweeter, so if you want to get intelligent tweets from someone interesting, she's the one to follow.

I also want to put a big shout out to Julianna Hinckley who edited many of these stories. She's in the process of editing the "big volume of shorts" I mentioned earlier, so it was just a fall out that some of her work would appear here. Thanks, Julianna, I don't know what I'd do without you.

As always, I want to thank my girlfriend, Shannon, for always being there (in her own little way), and my children for constantly putting up with me.

I should also mention my writing group, a nice

bunch of folk who let me bounce ideas off of them every two weeks. This one's for you, Chilliwack Writers' Group.

This truly is a "best of" book. I had a lot of short stories to choose from while putting it together (it's amazing how many shorts you write over a span of ten years or so) and I knew I wanted to keep it focused on the ones that shone, so I really did cherry pick my best. You might say, these are my "greatest hits." Some are award winners. Others went on to be in Year's Best anthologies.

In a nutshell, this is me at what *I* consider my best. Others may prefer different stories of mine than the ones I chose, I don't know, but the handful you're reading here, for whatever reason, are my personal favorites.

There's no theme running through the book, so don't bother looking for one. Science fiction stories have been thrown haphazardly together with stories about love or adventure. Nothing even comes in any particular order, other than this being the way I thought suited them best. In other words, you're pretty much left at my mercy.

Oh well, my stories, my rules. I hope you enjoy them. The stories, that is. Not the rules.

Without any further preamble, let's dip right in . . .

One of my favorite stories ever is *Daniel Keyes's* Flowers for Algernon. *I remember reading it in the fourth grade, and it was the first story that ever moved me.*

Well, my writing group, the Ram's Head, was having a party one summer and we were all supposed to write a summer-themed story to read at the party. I didn't remember until the night before, so I scrambled to get something written. I wrote all night, and went through three separate drafts. When I was finished, I had My Lame Summer Journal by Brandon Harris Grade 7. *I consider this my* Flowers for Algernon.

Interestingly, when I wrote my novel Dreams with Little Angels, *I wanted to write my own* To Kill a Mockingbird. *Little did I know that New York Times bestseller Deborah Crombie, in her endorsement of that book, would later compare my protagonist in the story to Harper Lee's Scout.*

My Lame Summer Journal
By Brandon Harris Grade 7

"This story is wonderful . . . Shades of Catcher in the Rye *and* Summer of '42, *yet with more subtle drama and tragedy than either one of them. The progression from laconic, semi-articulate disdain to hyperbolic overkill to stark, poetic simplicity is masterful and the characters are brilliant. The English teacher, Mr. Sanders, emerges clearly, without ever*

being described; the father is juxtaposed with Curley [from Of Mice and Men] *without a direct connection ever being made; and the looming tension of the entire piece never lets up, with the narrator's skills increasing exponentially as the overwhelming aura of inevitability gains momentum."*

- Jack Whyte, International Bestseller

"Not only a gripping story with an authentic voice, but a marvelous technical feat, combining **three** *separate stories taking place simultaneously. By turns funny, touching, and horrifying; a beautiful job."*

- Diana Gabaldon, New York Times Bestseller

July 10, Thursday

Okay, I'm starting this lame summer journal. I think it's very unfair to get homework over summer. Remember you said we wont get in trouble no matter what stuff we say. Nobody else got homework. Just because you changed to grade 7 and know the 6rs will be in your class again we got homework. Mom said it wasn't fair too but she told me to do it so I keep my good grades. She says you did it because you think we are smart and that is why we have to read the dumb book too. I wish I didn't tell her about the book. She keeps asking me if I started.

This journal won't be long that's for sure since I don't do much. That's why I waited til now to start it. So far this is what I did.

I played lots of Tony Hawk and Def Jam Vendetta. Mark Green lives five houses away and comes over a lot. I rule Tony Hawk. Mark blows. I don't think Mark started his journal yet. Marks little brother broke his Play Station 2 before school ended. His name is Timmy and he is a real little shit. Remember Mr. Sanders you said we could write anything. Bet you didn't think of that.

That's all I did. Mom is calling for dinner. Smells like chicken. I might write more later.

July 13, Sunday

We are at Grams for dinner and I'm writing this in Grampa's shed. He died two years ago and we come over every Sunday for a roast. Mom helps with house-work and Dad watches TV and drinks. Nobody comes in here anymore but I like it. Mom says Grampa used to hide in here to get away from Gram and that I'm like him but I don't know I don't remember him much.

Grandpa must have liked wine because he sure made lots that are still here. One wall is green bottles and they are all full there must be a thousand but I didn't count. Grampa liked guns too I guess and there are old guns on another wall in a case. Here is a secret. The case isn't locked because me and Brian broke it last summer but nobody knows. Brian broke it really. We put it back so it looks good. Besides you hardly can see in because the glass is so dirty. Grampa has three guns and they are old but I don't know what all of them are but Brian did. I think the small one is a Texas Ranger or some dumb ass name but the rest are different. They are bigger.

Brian is kind of my cousin but not really. His dad is my Uncle Ralph but I only call him my uncle he is not really my uncle. But I always called him Uncle. I don't know why. They live in Fort Nelson where Gram and Grampa used to live and Dad too and they come in the summers and stay a week.

I'm sitting at Grampa's desk. It's why this paper is so dirty (sorry Mr. Sanders) because the desk is dirty. Brian and me found bullets in the drawer last year and I just checked and some are still there. We got in trouble because we took them down to the tracks to see if the train would make them shoot off. It was mostly Brian's idea but Dad gave me a whooping like crazy because I told him it was me too because Mom says you should never lie. If you lie you will get eaten up by the guilt and I think Mom is probably right.

I never got to see the train come.

That reminds me. Brian and Uncle Ralph are supposed to come soon I think in two weeks. I might have some good stuff to write then because he never wants to play PS2 like Mark. They don't play much PS2 in Fort Nelson.

Dad is yelling for me I have to stop I will try to write more later.

Okay I'm back and it's night and I'm in bed. Nothing much happened. Dad was fighting with Mom at Gram's and we had to go and they yelled all the way home in the car. I thought it would be good to start the book but I left it at home. Now its beside my bed.

July 17, Thursday

I just had a fight with Mark and told him to go home. I was beating his ass at SSX Tricky and he rebooted the PS2 so I lost my high score in the middle of a game. He is such a baby. I was bored of him being here all the time too but his mom said they cant afford to fix his PS2 so now he is SOL. That means shit out of luck. You said we could write any stuff. I bet you didn't think that.

I looked at the book today. At least its not so big. I sometimes think it will be neat if I do read it because I never read a real book all the way. I started Harry Potter once but only read a little and then the movie came out so I didn't have to. Too bad there wasn't a movie about Mice and Men then I could just pretend I read it. Just joking Mr. Sanders.

I'm going to try and read some after supper but I have to rake the lawn first because Dad told me two times and said the third one is the belt. He is home from work today and drinking and I know I better rake or get a wooping.

Okay, I'm back. Miss me? I'm in bed writing this. I just finished raking and had my bath and it's dark outside it took so long and Dad isn't happy but at least I didn't get the belt. I'm going to stop writing this and start Mice and Men so bye.

July 18, Friday

I read the first chapter!!!!! It took hours and I'm tired but I can't believe you Mr. Sanders. I think you like swear words because there were lots in the book. God damn and bastard and son-of-a-bitch but lots of god damns. I think it's a pretty good book I like the guy named Lennie because he always does things wrong and doesn't mean to and his friend George helps him. George tells him guys like us give a damn about us and makes Lennie feel better and says one day they will have a garden with rabbits and that makes Lennie happy. See, Mr. Sanders I did read it. You probably thought I was joking. I even looked up some stuff because when I woke up I asked my mom where some places are like Soledad and what some words mean and she said well I don't have time to be your god damn dictionary. I laughed when she said god damn because it's in the book so much but don't worry Mr. Sanders I never said that to her.

She got me an atlas and a dictionary. They were in the closet under the stairs that is so full of junk Dad can never find anything in it.

Did you know that Soledad is a city in northern columbia and the Salinas River is in montery and the Gabilan mountains is in Gonzales? And a sycamore is any of various deciduous trees of the genus platanus.

There is no word called bindle so I think the book made a mistake but then it might be like when Lennie talks with not real words like on'y when he means only. I didn't understand that at all at first but then I figured it out. I think bindle is supposed to be bundle. You learn something new every day but I'm still not sure what a sycamore is. I will ask Mom later when she's not washing the kitchen floor I tracked mud on and her soaps aren't on TV.

It's ten minutes later now and I just looked at all the stuff I wrote and can't believe how long it is. This is probably the longest journal ever and ha ha you have to read it because you made us do homework over the summer Mr. Sanders. I bet you never thought that.

July 20, Sunday

I finished chapter two. It was harder than the first because parts don't make sense even when I read them twice. Lennie and George got a job and most people there are nice but the guy called Curley is mean. I think he will hurt Lennie but Lennie has George to beat him up after so that's okay.

The chapter made Dad slap me because of some of the words I didn't know and he heard me ask Mom. He said I was a mouthy little son-of-a-bitch. I won't say it again ever and I don't think it should be used so many times in a book chapter if it gets you slapped for asking. I will tell you because we have a deal. It is nigger and I still don't really know what it means because when I looked in the dictionary it said a disparaging term for a member of a deprived group of people and I had to look up disparaging and soon I just didn't care as long as I didn't get slapped again. The dictionary is a god damn bastard and John Steinbeck is a son-of-a-bitch. Just joking Mr. Sanders.

July 26, Saturday

Guess what I just found out? That Brian and uncle Ralph came down last Thursday and nobody told me. They are at Grams and we are going tomorrow as usual and they will probably come back here after and stay a couple of days. It will be fun because me and him and Jolene get to sleep in the living room. Oh yeah I don't think I told about Jolene before. She is Brian's sister and she is older and pretends we don't exist. I'm not sure how old.

I just asked Mom and Jolene is going into grade 11 and Brian is going into grade 8 but he is supposed to go to grade 9 but he flunked out grade 5. But he never has no homework on summer holidays that's for sure. I'm just joking Mr. Sanders.

Mom was wearing lots of makeup and it was running because I think Mom was crying or something but she didn't want me to know so I didn't ask but I told her about Lennie and George's garden with rabbits and that we are lucky because we give a damn about us and that seemed to cheer her up.

July 27, Sunday

Went to Grams for dinner. Brian and Jolene and my uncle Ralph was there but they didn't come back here like I thought. They are gonna come tomorrow and Dad isn't going to work for it. Mom said it made her happy that it wasn't til tomorrow they would come and Dad said she was an unsociable bitch he was drunk and they were already fighting like you will see.

Brian is going into grade 8 and told me sometimes they do stuff when you start grade 8 like beat you up or stick your head in the toilet. I think he is scared. My dad said when he went to grade 8 they tied some kid to a tree and he stayed there for the night and a grizzly bear ate him. They only wanted to tie him there for a bit to scare him but they all forgot. I wonder if maybe they tied him to a sycamore? I know what sycamore is now, Mr. Sanders. It is a tree and looks like a normal tree. Anyway Mom told Dad to shut up because he was drunk and making it up. Uncle Ralph said no it happened for real but he was drunk too. Everyone started fighting loud. Brian got a beer and nobody saw. We took it out to the shed and shared it and then Brian opened one of Grampa's wine with a screwdriver and had some of that too. I only had a little.

Brian opened the gun cupboard and the Texas Ranger was gone and he guessed Gram traded it for booze.

Jolene came out too. She had wine too. She was wearing a shirt with a horse on it and her boobs were really big. She didn't have them last summer I'm sure at least not so big if she did. Bet you didn't think I'd write that did you Mr. Sanders?

I read Of Mice And Men when we drove home while Mom and Dad yelled. Tomorrow I think Brian and Jolene will stay for two days.

July 28, Monday

I'm writing this on the floor in my sleeping bag. Uncle
Ralph is sleeping in my bed and me and Brian get the
floor in the living room. It's two twenty on the VCR but
it's fast ten minutes or so. Jolene is on the couch. Her
and Brian are asleep and Brian snores that is probably
why I'm awake. Brian took vodka from the kitchen and
nobody saw there was so much they thought they just
drunk it. Him and Jolene drank it with Coke. I had a
little bit. Jolene wears a big blue shirt with 21 on it to
sleep and she passed out and Brian made me lift up her
shirt and see her boobs. They are real big but I only saw
a minute because she moved and I thought she was
gonna wake up and catch me I was scared. Brian just
laughed. He had some beer and then he went to sleep
and snored. We didn't go down to the creek or outside
at all and of course we didn't play any PS2 because they
don't in Fort Nelson. It was fun last year when we used
to go down to the bog and sometimes play flag football
in the grass field at the school. I can't believe Jolene's
boobs got so much bigger since then.

I just heard something break in the kitchen and
everybody is yelling so I better stop now and go to sleep.
Tomorrow we are gonna go down to the bog. I hope
Jolene comes.

July 29, Tuesday

Brian was too sick to go to the bog. Me and Jolene just
went and it was weird. We sat on a log and she drew

stuff in the dirt with a stick. Then she smoked. She told me not to tell. I said I wouldn't. She told me she wasn't really asleep last night when I lifted up her shirt. I felt dumb but she said it was okay. She has blonde hair and blue eyes and red lips and blue fingernails. She asked me if I have a girlfriend. I shook my head and she asked me if I have done stuff with a girl. I felt dumb and shaky but she said it was okay. She asked me if I liked her boobs. I said I think they are bigger this summer and she laughed and that made me feel better.

Then she asked if I wanted to see them again. I looked around the bog but nobody else was there. I heard the frogs and nodded but she wanted me to say yes. "Say it" she said so I said yes and my voice squeaked. "Louder" she said. "Tell me you want to see my boobs."

So I said "I want to" and she took her shirt right off and had a white bra on. I looked around again but still it was only me and the frogs and Jolene and her bra. Then she undid the bra and they were so big and I felt dumb.

"Do you like them?" she said. I nodded and then said "yes I like them" because I knew she was going to tell me to say it if I didn't. I still felt dumb but then she smiled and I felt better. She said I can touch them and did I want to and I said yes right away so she wouldn't think I didn't like them. My hand was shaking like crazy I felt so dumb but guess what happened? I never touched them because a god damn bastard of two dogs ran out of the bush. They barked like a son-of-a-bitch and scared us and Jolene threw her cigarette into the bog and put her shirt back on. It was smart because a man I guess was walking the dogs came out in a minute. He reminded me of Curley from Of Mice And Men because he wrecked it like Curley always does.

Jolene and Brian and Uncle Ralph went back to Fort Nelson today. They decided to stay just one night. Brian was still sick. Uncle Ralph shook my hand and gave me five bucks like he always does and Mom told me to give it back and that I didn't deserve it and that he shouldn't give me money. She says the same thing every year they come down and everyone knows I'm not giving back the money so I think it's just a waste of time but I don't care. Mom wastes time a lot. Maybe you should give her a book to read, Mr. Sanders.

Jolene stared at me and blew a kiss when they drove away Mom never saw and Dad was still in bed. He was sick too and has to go back to work tomorrow.

Mom just told me she is going to bed and that nothing is better than when relatives finally go home which is funny since Ralph isn't really my uncle but Mom is strange sometimes. She found the empty vodka bottle in the living room and asked me if Brian or Jolene was drinking and I said no I didn't think so but then I said yes they were because I was feeling the guilt start to eat me. I don't think she will tell Dad.

I don't miss Brian at all. All I can think of is Jolene and how she had no boobs last time and now they were so big. I miss Jolene a lot.

July 31, Thursday

I got my cast off today! Oh I guess you didn't know about the cast because I never said about it but I had a cast because I broke my arm when I fell off the fence. The doctor took it off and I'm happy even though my arm looks like a baby's arm except worse. More like a tree branch maybe. Oh well its supposed to be normal soon. The doctor asked if I wanted to keep the cast since Mark and my Mom and some other people wrote stuff on it but Mom said no Dad wouldn't want us to bring it home because I didn't fall off the fence like Mom told the doctor. Dad broke my arm by accident when he grabbed it too hard after I dumped lemonade all over the counter because I didn't hold the top on. I'm god damn dumb sometimes.

I told the doctor I didn't want the cast anyways unless it came with a garden and rabbits and he looked at me like I was a god damn crazy bastard but Mom laughed and that made me glad I said it.

August 4, Monday

Mom told me I should stop fighting with Mark and I thought so too because you need guys like Mark who give damns about you. I went to Mark's house and I even gave him my PS2 on a loan because I'm not playing it these days and he needs the practice more than me because of how much he blows at Tony Hawk. He was happy as could be and it made me happy that he was. I got home and told Mom and she got happy too. I think maybe happy is catchy.

I don't think Mark started his summer homework yet because I asked if he wanted to come down to the bog with me and he said he cant because his Mom wont let him until he starts his homework. He maybe just wanted to play with my PS2.

I have to go the police are here. I will try to write more later.

August 5, Tuesday

I don't like Curley. He is mean and hurts people because he likes it. I hope Lennie punches him in the god damn face but he won't because he is too nice. I like Curley's wife because she reminds me of Jolene and she is nice too and its not her fault she married a son-of-a-bitch like Curley.

The police came over last night and I thought they wanted to see Dad and I think Dad did too but they went to all the houses and talked because somebody heard gunshots or something. I hoped they didn't make Dad mad like they do sometimes when they come and they didn't but I think Mom was worried about that to. She was shaky after.

I think John Steinbeck must be a millionaire because of how good of books he writes. I bet he lives in a big house with a garden and rabbits and that is why he writes that Lennie likes them so much. I'm going to write like John Steinbeck and be a millionaire and buy a house for my Mom and me. I'm on page 80 but reading slower now since I want to learn.

August 6, Wednesday

I articulated to Mom that I ambitioned to be a prodigious wordsmith like John Steinbeck and she vocalized that to do that I would requisite to cognize supplementary words. She lavished upon me a thesaurus.

I envisage my scripture is getting massingly professional. I fugacious to inquire Mom what she manifested, but I unrecalled the news was on and Dad got massingly splenetic at me for making cacophony and so I went perpendicular to bed abstained any principal nourishment. It is god damn astonishing how god damn dumb I can be sometimes.

August 7, Thursday

Curiously Mom stopped washing dishes in the wet water and wiped her wet hands on her pinkish apron with a red tie that I gave her for Christmas last year and she said she really liked. Excitement flowed through me as my hand gave her my journal so she could see my writing.

Her voice sounded like music and she said, "It's not about big words. It's the way you use the words you pick."

I glanced at the snow white paper she was holding and then up to her big brown eyes and bruised face and thought she was right. John Steinbeck used simple words that are easy but he makes them sound like beautiful poetry, like doves flapping their wings. A warm, summer blew in the window and I smelled fresh mowed lawn.

"And," she said, tossing her soft, dark hair, "you need to learn about grammar and punctuation too."

The day had begun.

August 8, Friday

Being a millionaire writer like John Steinbeck is harder than you think. I think it might take weeks until I'm even close to being good enough to put out a book. Probably even more before I can write a really good one like Of Mice And Men. So, for now, I will go back to writing my old, lame way. The good part about deciding this is that I get to go back to reading the rest of the book.

I have to go now. Dad just got home from work early and he is really mad. I will try to write more later.

August 11, Monday

I couldn't write until now since Mom went to the hospital Friday after Dad punched her in the stomach and she was coughing blood. She told the doctors that she fell down some stairs but I don't think they believed her. She called and asked my aunt Tina if I could stay at her place until she got out of the hospital because she didn't want me to be home alone with Dad so that is why I haven't written anything. When I came out and saw Mom bleeding I grabbed her arm and ran her to the neighbors who drove her to the hospital. I didn't have time to come back for my journal or John Steinbeck.

Dad lost his job Friday. I don't know why, only that he is very angry. Mom and I are both staying out of his way. If I were five years older and stronger, I swear I would kill that god damn son-of-a-bitch.

I tried to read now that I'm home but I can't follow much. I'm worried about Mom.

August 12, Tuesday

I'm sitting in the backseat of the car and we're going camping. Dad suddenly decided camping was very important. I think he is very drunk. Mom has not stopped crying since she got out of the hospital and I keep seeing new bruises on her and I'm afraid. I look into her eyes and I'm scared because I don't see her anymore looking back. She looks like a wild animal and I have no idea where we are going but there is lots of trees everywhere and not many cars go by and it is getting dark outside.

I have read a little to think of something else instead of camping. I don't think Curley's wife is that nice anymore because when she was being nice to Lennie I think she should have known what would happen. I only have one chapter left.

We are stopping so I will put my journal away. This place doesn't look like a camp site to me but Dad says we're here.

August 12, Tuesday / Night

Why Mr. Sanders? All that time I spent reading was for what reason? I don't understand why did George kill Lennie? Curley deserved to be killed, not Lennie. Lennie was supposed to get a garden with rabbits.

It is an awful story. I hate Of Mice And Men and I hate John Steinbeck.

I'm in the woods and I'm alone and scared and I have my backpack that I brought my journal and Of Mice And Men in and I also brought something else that I never told you about before. It wasn't a big secret and Gram never uses it so the guilt didn't eat me except I just didn't know why I took it so I didn't know how to write it or I would.

Remember when Brian saw the missing gun in Grampa's shed? Well he was wrong. Gram didn't trade the Texas Ranger for booze or anything because I took it home with me and two bullets from the top drawer. Last week I took it down to the bog and figured out how to shoot it and that leaves one bullet and I just put it in the gun. It was hard because I kept dropping the bullet my hand is shaking so much. I'm so scared Mr. Sanders.

We got here an hour ago maybe and the first thing Dad did was make a huge bonfire that I can still hear and Dad was calmer but not me. I was mad like crazy and he made me do stuff with the tent and the fire and I got madder than I ever was before.

Then I did the biggest god damn dumb thing ever. Dad threw me the end of the string for the tent and told me to "tie it to that Douglas Fir" and then I did the thing. I couldn't stop myself and I knew Dad was going to kill us I made him so mad.

"It's not a god damn Douglas fir you stupid son-of-a-bitch," I said. "It's a god damn sycamore."

Then I wasn't angry no more I was just scared and cried and Dad picked up the hammer and came at me but Mom grabbed him and she screamed at me to run away. I saw the end of the hammer hit her head and she was bleeding and I grabbed my backpack and ran into the woods. Mom screamed and screamed but I don't hear her anymore only that god damn fire.

I'm not strong and I'm really scared. I hope you can read this my hand is shaking so much and I know Dad's hands don't shake and he is stronger and he isn't scared. And he is coming.

I read the last chapter just now because I didn't know what to do and I had the book in my backpack so I read about George killing Lennie and now I wonder why you would want to read something as horrible as real life.

Lennie's rabbits made me happy but John Steinbeck killed them like he killed Lennie.

I'm trying to think of any happy part in the end and all I can is that maybe it is that Lennie was killed by someone who gave a damn about him instead of that bastard Curley. Guys like us are different because we give a damn so much I will kill you even though it will hurt me so you die with dignity.

Is that what the ending means, Mr. Sanders?

I can hear him and I'm scared he's close.

I have to go now, Mr. Sanders.

I hope your summer was better than mine.

You know something else? They did make a movie but I decided to read the book instead because people always say the movie isn't as good and you know what? I think they are probably right. I know what I have to do.

Goodbye Mr. Sanders.

Brandon H.

The end.

I've always been fascinated by Lewis Carroll and knew one day I'd write an homage to him. Little did I know it would come in the form of his famous "Jabberwocky" poem or that it would feature Nikola Tesla (another favorite of mine). I had to do a bit of time juggling to have all these people actually appear in the same story, but hopefully nobody notices that. I think the final outcome was well worth the artistic license. Oh, and just in case anybody's wondering, the odd contraction syntax on can't (ca'n't) is intentional—it's the way Carroll and a few—a rather small few—other authors of his day tried to foist the contraction as being the status quo. Needless to say, they were unsuccessful. Still, I leave his technique here, full and intact, as a tribute to a man who makes less and less sense the harder you try to understand him . . .

The Reality of Time

"Michael Hiebert has a positive flair for concocting wonderful tales out of things that should not go together. Love, death, and dying, creatures (and vorpal blades) out of Carroll's 'Jabberwocky' poem, and one of the greatest (and most controversial) inventors of the latter Victorian era all swirl into a marvelous coming of age tale in, The Reality of Time.*"*
- Julianna Hinckley, author of Taminah.

When I remember my childhood days in England, I recall them being filled with happy, callow afternoons playing with my older brother Harry. It's always summer, always around midday, and always warm and bright.

I know that ca'n't be how it really was, but time has a peculiar way of changing things. To be honest, I don't particularly mind remembering everything this way.

Harry and I would frolic about the garden those endless afternoons, usually engaged in sword play using short swords our father constructed from two pieces of wood; a long one that came to a dull point for the blade, and a short one nailed across, forming the guard of the hilt.

We left them unpainted. Paint was as unnecessary as the castle wall we battled precariously atop, thrusting and parrying between mother's rose bushes and the clutch of daisies beside the steps.

"Take that," I would say, lunging at my brother.

With a clever turn of his wrist, Harry would block. "Arthur!" Usually, he called me Arty, but at these times always it was Arthur. I suspect for the medieval knight-liness my full name evoked. "You must take me a fool, trying such tricks!" He would follow with something fancy; perhaps a spin and a backhand slash. Almost always, the fancy moves tripped him up, and we would both laugh.

We lived in the town of Godstow, just north of Oxford and west of the river Isis, and my memories of that time are mostly yellow. Happy, sunny, yellow.

Eventually, though, that time passed on, the way time always does. The colors in my memory shift then, from yellow to deep scarlet. Feverish, deathly, scarlet. Back then we called it *Scarlatina*.

It took Mum first. Then, a fortnight later, it came for Harry.

Until that time, Father had been a successful man of business. Even at my young age, however, I suspected deep down he possessed a buried lust for adventure. You saw it sparkle in his eyes when he read stories about David Livingstone heading to Africa to source the river Nile, or Henry Morton Stanley being dispatched to go find him after Livingstone's mysterious six year disappearance.

When Mum and Harry died, Father exhumed his dream of adventure and, within months, decided he and I would travel across Europe.

"What about school?" I asked.

"You ca'n't possibly believe a boy can learn more in school than he can looking at the world first hand!" He laughed, but I felt there was something stronger than just whimsy pushing his decision.

Those were days of tremendous change. The expansion of power and wealth sweeping through England attracted the envy of other nations. Europe was in flux. Already, Britain was struggling for strategic parts of Africa. The Prussians had just invaded France. And there was more than a little worry their eyes may now be looking across toward England.

I think, having lost the rest of his family, Father worried about my personal safety, and that worry played a significant role in his plans.

We sold the cottage and most of our belongings. What little we kept, we packed into portmanteaus. Father's was black and heavily worn from numerous business trips. Mine was burgundy, unused, and smaller, but everything I owned fit inside. The only items I considered precious were the wooden swords Father made for Harry and me, and a letter from Mum that Father presented me with upon her death; a sad thing she wrote while sick, telling me how she knew I would grow up to make her ever so proud, and that she would continue to watch over me the rest of my life.

Father booked us passage to France, and arranged for a trip by railroad that would ultimately take us to Rome. "We'll plan the rest from there," he said.

I kept a jar in my room which held my entire life's savings. Before we left, I dumped it out, stuffing the money into the pocket of my trousers. Eighteen shillings.

In the days leading up to our departure, I noticed Father did not seem his regular self. When I asked him if he felt ill, he said, "No, I'm right perfect. Tip-top!" I suppose, having sold everything we owned, and already paid out a large sum, feeling any other way was pointless.

But he grew worse quickly and, by the time our boat reached Northern France, Father could no longer pretend he felt tip-top. He spent most of the voyage in the lavatory. As we queued to disembark, his entire body trembled as I watched him struggle to lift his portmanteau. His body glistened with sweat. His hair was wet with it. He managed to wobble off the boat, but by the time we were to board the train, he could barely stand on his feet.

I handed the conductor our tickets. With one look at Father, he handed them right back refusing to allow us on. Despite every effort to persuade him, I eventually watched the train chug away while propping up Father beside the tracks.

Struggling, I approached a carriage man. "My father is very ill," I said. "He needs a bed."

He looked up. "*Eh? Je parle seulement anglais.*"

I knew enough French to ask again in a manner he understood.

Pressing his finger to his lips, the man in the black top hat thought a moment then snapped his fingers. "Aha! I know a place."

"They have rooms available?"

He nodded. "Rooms."

He loaded our bags and helped me with Father. Then I realized something. "I've no francs," I said.

This, he understood immediately. "You have pounds?"

I pulled the coins from my pocket. "I've eighteen shillings."

Frowning, he considered the money in my palm. Finally he took it. "Place we go is close enough."

I climbed inside and he closed the door. Father slumped on the bench across from me, barely conscious, leaving me making adult decisions. With a jerk, the vehicle began moving. The horses clopped, the wheels crunched, and panic battled inside me.

It was a two story, red brick house and, according to the painted wooden sign, called *Le Petit Lapin*. Surrounding it was a dense wood that brought me an uneasy feeling of isolation as I stepped down from the carriage. During the short trip, dusk had crept in, bringing with it a bruised and cloudy sky. A warm summer wind smelling sweetly of roses blew across my face.

A woman and her daughter greeted us. The woman was portly, with chestnut hair wrapped in curl papers. She spoke no English, but the driver explained Father was ill and needed a bed.

"*Pouvez-vous me donner l'argent?*" she asked me.

"Yes, I have money," I assured her. "I just have to find it."

Not understanding, she turned to her daughter. "Amabelle?"

Amabelle had long straight hair and fringe the same color as her mum. Freckles splashed across her cheeks. "*Oui, maman,*" she said, and translated my words.

Amabelle introduced her mum as Mrs. Renoir. Mrs. Renoir showed us to our room upstairs, and the driver was kind enough to help with Father and the bags. The house had three rooms for let, and we were given number two—a modest space with a single bed, an unpainted chest of drawers, and a dressing mirror. The wooden floor I was to sleep on was uneven, but I didn't worry as Amabelle fetched an extra blankets and pillow for me. I felt exhausted enough to have slept on nails.

Mrs. Renoir brought a steel bucket of water and a white rag and set it beside Father's bed. "For his fever," Amabelle explained. Her mother crossed the room and opened the window slightly. "Fresh air," Amabelle explained further. Mrs. Renoir then told me a doctor would arrive in the morning. I started to thank her, but Amabelle interrupted to translate for me.

"*Merci*," I said.

That night, my father's fever induced delirium.

I woke to his voice straining to call me. "My son . . . " he whispered. My heart leapt as I thought his fever had broken, but, as I clamored to his bedside, my hope quickly fell away. His eyes closed, he still slept as his whispering continued on nonsensically. " . . . watch the Bandersnatch as you feed the borogroves." Or, at least, that's how it sounded to me.

I dipped the rag Mrs. Renoir had left in the bucket of cool water, and held it against his forehead, fearing the heat I felt rising from his skin. The compress helped a little and he soon fell quiet again. I returned to the floor consumed in worry, unable to sleep. How many hours I spent staring at the ceiling, I don't know. Eventually, I started to nod off.

A loud crack in the night sent my pulse racing. My eyes snapped open as a white flash outside my window filled the room as brightly as though it were daytime. Nervously, I stood and crept across the floor. The window overlooked the garden where, farther back, a barn nestled amongst the woods. The barn's doors were open and, as I watched, lightning again erupted inside the building, ripping the peaceful night apart. Hot, electric light flashed with such intensity, I had to shield my eyes with my hand until it died away.

I continued to stand by the window and watch the barn for some time, but the phenomenon never repeated. Eventually, I returned to my bed and fell into a fitful sleep.

When the doctor arrived the next morning, Mrs. Renoir suggested I go outside in the garden while he inspected my father. Even though I understood, Amabelle translated anyway. I considered telling her it wasn't needed, but, realizing how much she enjoyed doing it, decided to just let her continue. She was at least three years younger than me and, for her age, spoke English very well. I found her rather comely.

I followed Amabelle downstairs. We went outside through the back door in the kitchen, which stepped down onto a stone porch. Although the garden was in serious neglect, it appeared to have been well-kept at one time. A stone bridge arched over a narrow brook, and a path that curved around raised areas of ground. These were perhaps once planted and well-tended, but had now been taken over by wildflowers.

The property eventually pushed back against a lush forest, forming a wall of green that towered well above the roof of Mrs. Renoir's house. The trees were mostly evergreens with brown trunks, knotty and thick. Squatting between them, almost as tall as the house, was the barn I saw from my bedroom window. In the pale thin light of morning, it looked simply dilapidated and grotty, weathered by time. The front doors were closed, secured with a rusty chain and padlock. Compared to what I saw last night, it seemed asleep.

Amabelle skipped ahead of me, wearing a threadbare blue and white pinafore. We were headed toward the woods, where Amabelle assured me we'd find a trail. The barn kept tugging at my attention. Time had faded its wooden siding to a sickly almost-white pallor. In some places, the wind had blown the planks completely off the wall, leaving spaces that revealed the barn's dark interior. As we skulked past, I tried to pull details from out of the shadows, but had little success.

Then, something *did* catch my eye.

I paused and peered harder, narrowing my eyes. The roof must also have had wood missing in places, allowing sunlight to cast down through the holes. Inside, the sunlight's reflection twinkled in something hidden in the darkness. Something metallic, I thought.

Amabelle noticed I'd stopped walking. She stomped back. "That is where *le professeur* works. We're not . . . " She searched for the English word. " . . . *supposed* to go near. Even when he is . . . even when he is not out here."

"The professor?"

"*Oui*. He is in room number three."

"What does he do out here?"

With a shrug, Amabelle grabbed my hand and pulled for me to continue toward the woods. "Come! I want you to meet someones."

I gave the barn one last glance before letting her tow me to the edge of the garden then down a trail. Not far into the woods, the trail opened into a small circular clearing with a stump of extraordinary width rooted nearly dead center. This looked to have once been part of the garden, probably furnished with potted plants.

Now, all that remained were broken pieces of clay scattered about. Two sundials still stood on either side of the stump. They had large chips in their columns, and time had faded them gray.

Amabelle pushed herself up onto the stump, and sat dangling her legs. She patted the place beside her. "You sit here."

I did, slightly more careful than she about getting my clothes dirty.

"Now we must be very quiet," she said.

"Why?" I asked, but she held her finger to her lips, shushing me. I made no noise, but mocked her with funny faces. Rocking my head from side to side, I lifted my eyes in exaggerated anticipation.

"Stop it!" She walloped me in the stomach. "Stop it! Just sit . . . *comme une personne normale!*"

"And how, may I ask, does a normal person sit?"

She shushed me again, then pointed by a tangle of bushes at the edge of the clearing. "Look," she whispered. "*Voila*. See?"

The most curious creature stepped out from the woods.

At first I thought it a stork. It stood on long, thin legs, ending in chicken feet. But, even for a stork, the legs seemed much too long. And though the rest of it did indeed resemble a bird, there was nothing stork-like about it. The top of the legs protruded from a plumed ball of wispy feathers colored an odd assortment of lemon, lime, and rust. A beak, painted in these same colors, stuck out one end, and was banana-shaped, like the beaks of toucans I'd seen drawn in books.

I slowly leaned forward, not wanting to startle the creature. "It's amazing," I whispered. Quickly, the angle of the beak changed, as though it were cocking an eye at us, an eye hidden within all those feathers.

Proudly beaming, Amabelle said, "It is a borogrove!"

I knew I'd heard that word before, but it took a moment for me to remember it was during the night while Father was delirious. *Watch the Bandersnatch as you feed the borogroves.*

"Is that a French word?" I asked.

"No," she said, "It is not any kind of word. Just a name."

"I . . . I don't understand."

But her attention drifted back to the borogrove, squealing gleefully as two new animals bounded from the edge of the woods. These were much smaller, more like hares. Indeed, at first I thought they *were* hares. They had long floppy ears and hareish faces. It was there, though, that the similarity ended. Their chubby bodies were wrapped in leathery puce skin instead of fluffy fur and they ended in twisty tails. Even after the borogrove, they were most remarkable.

Amabelle clapped her hands. "Raths! *Je les adore absolument!*"

The sudden appearance of the raths around its feet nearly tripped up the borogrove. It had to perform a little dance by lifting first one foot, then the other, bending its thin legs at the knee to do so. Amabelle laughed as twice it almost stumbled as the raths hopped beneath it. "They make the borogrove mimsy," she said.

Raths and mimsy were more words I didn't know and, like borogrove, they didn't sound French.

With a grunt, the smaller of the two raths lifted its head and howled. The howl started like a quiet train whistle, growing louder as it went. Halfway through, it belched so it could refill its lungs with enough air to finish.

"That is its outgrabe," Amabelle said. "It is calling for its *mère* ."

Sure enough, from off in the distant trees some-where, the same sound echoed back, only with a slightly different pitch.

I looked at Amabelle. "All these words. Where did you learn them?"

"I dreamed them."

From the other side of the garden, Mrs. Renoir called for us to return to the house. Her voice scared the borogrove. Awkwardly, it marched into the trees, avoiding the raths hopping and scurrying beneath it.

Amabelle frowned. "You did not meet them all."

"There're more?" I asked, astounded.

She jumped down and showed me the hollowed out ground beneath one of the sundials. "That's a wabe. It's their . . . " She struggled unsuccessfully for the English word. " . . . their *nid*."

I hadn't known wabe, but I knew *nid*. "Their nest? *Whose* nest?"

She straightened her pinafore and brushed it off. "The toves. But they sleep here only in night." With a wave, she gestured deeper into the woods. "They are out there now, hiding."

"Hiding from what?"

Her voice dropped to a whisper. "Le Bandersnatch." Then, with a grin, she yelled, "Let us race back!" and bolted toward the house, leaving me alone with the uneasy memory of Father's midnight rambling.

The doctor left Father some tablets and said the best thing for him now was rest. So, after giving him his medicine in the afternoon, I took the wooden swords from my portmanteau and went in search of Amabelle. She'd never be a replacement for Harry, but with practice she might learn enough to be a welcome distraction.

She wasn't in her room beside Mrs. Renoir's on the bottom floor. I also didn't find her in the drawing room, which had a vaulted ceiling and a brick fireplace that covered an entire wall, all the way up to the top of the second story.

I suspected she was probably back on her stump in the clearing, watching her curious animal mates. Returning to the garden, I started toward the trail when I noticed the barn door chain was unlocked. Through the crack between the doors, I saw someone moving inside. It was the professor! Quietly, I snuck to the side of the barn and sat on my knees, peering in through a crack in the wall.

I gasped.

Giant apparatus filled the barn. At one end, thin black legs arched from the floor supporting a silver sphere, its surface mirror-polished. At the other end, a silver corkscrew, also supported by thin legs, leaned toward the sphere. Its base as big as a carriage, it tapered to a point just below the barn's rafters.

Between these, a third piece of equipment hung from the central ceiling beam by steel wires. It was constructed from cobalt blue cubes, each one about the size of a jack-in-the-box, and they framed an oddly shaped chunky ring approximately a yard in diameter.

A thick trunk of black cables ran from the bottom of the corkscrew to a waist-high box set into the dirt floor of the barn. The box had a lever on one side, and two gauges and a row of buttons fixed into its top. Inside the box, a confused knot of colored wires ran every which way imaginable.

Normally, these wires were hidden by a removable front panel. I knew this because the professor squatted with most of his back to me, replacing this panel as I looked on. Once he secured the panel, he stood, turned in my direction, shot his cuffs, and adjusted his tie. He brushed dust from the sleeves of his neatly pressed navy suit. His hair was dark and thick, and he had a moustache.

His eyes were almost as dark as his hair. I realized too late they were looking straight into mine.

I barely had time to get to my feet before he was outside. "What are you doing out here?" He spoke English, with a thick Eastern European accent. At the time, I thought he might be Polish, or even Russian. I know now he came from Serbia.

"I . . . I . . . " With no real answer, I looked down at the swords in my hands.

Seeing them, he smiled. "Oh, well. Then of course." With an elaborate sweep of his arm he gestured toward the open garden. "Go on then. Show me your swordsmanship. Let me see how fine a fencer you are."

I set one sword down beside the barn, and, nervously, thrust and parried for him with the other. I had practiced doing so by myself many times, but it felt awkward in front of a stranger.

He picked the other sword up off the ground and looked me over, head to toe. "You are filthy. You must give more attention to your hygiene. Now, *en garde*!" His sword hand thrust forward, his other rested on his hip.

The professor proved to be a much better swordsman than either Harry or I could ever have hoped to be. Even with Father's mere wooden play swords, his talent was obvious. He easily evaded all of my attacks, and, after letting me block a few of his strikes, he finally stabbed me, touching the dull wooden point gingerly to my throat.

"And that, sir, is your demise," he laughed. "But you show promise," he said, handing me back the sword, hilt first. After I took it, he carefully wiped his hands clean, meticulously picking out any dirt before returning to the barn.

Nervously, I followed, stopping at the door. "What is this?" From here, the apparatus felt even more monstrous.

He pushed a button on the box. "A bridge."

"What kind of bridge?"

"Between realities. Between the conscious and the vorpal."

Cautiously, I took a step inside. Looking up at the tip of the corkscrew, I felt tiny. "What's the vorpal?"

He tapped first one gauge, then the other. "The temporal vortex. You see it's like a portmanteau—there are two meanings packed up into one word. The temporal vortex is the reality of the subconscious."

"I don't understand."

"Where our mind sometimes visits when we sleep."

"You mean where our dreams are?"

Tapping the first gauge again, he nodded.

"It's a *real* place?"

Regarding me, he upturned his palm. "It is no more or less real than all this. Indeed, in a way, it is *more* real. But our waking minds are not aware of it. This machine searches for instances when a bridge between both realities is possible and tries to build one." He pulled the lever, with a clunk. A low humming filled he barn.

"How can it be *more* real?"

"Because vorpal matter is the stronger. Conscious matter cannot affect vorpal matter, but the reverse is not true."

"Still, I don't understand."

"Your swords? They could harm nothing vorpal. But a *vorpal sword*?" He made a slicing motion across his neck with his hand, then turned his attention to the sphere. Small static charges began forming on its surface. They buzzed for an instant, then disappeared.

"So is this where the strange animals in the woods come from?" I asked.

He nodded. "I have had limited success, but I am on the cusp of sustaining a stable link."

I watched as a long charged sizzled from the bottom of the corkscrew, fizzling out as it wound up to the rafters. "Why are you're building this bridge?"

He looked at me. *"Why?* Why do we attempt *anything*? To gain knowledge. To further ourselves." He tapped the gauge. "And also so I might patent and profit, of course."

Suddenly, above my head a huge blast erupted from the corkscrew, chilling me with fright. With a crack, the jolt leapt from the end of the coil, sailed through the co-balt ring of cubes, and attacked the sphere in a frenzy of static, encasing it briefly in a crazy ball of electricity before it sizzled out.

The professor frowned. "Always it breaks down."

My heart thumped so fast I could feel it behind my eyes. I swallowed. "I'm going to go now," I said, and left.

My nerves had calmed somewhat by the time I found Amabelle in the clearing. She brightened when she saw me approach. "You have arrived just in time. It is nearly brillig!"

I held up the swords. "I want to teach you to fence."

She stuck out her tongue. "Swords are for boys."

"They most certainly are not," I started, but she shushed me, and motioned me to sit. Anxiously she pointed at two odd faces peering out from the brush, cautiously surveying the area. Covered in fur, they were mostly white, with black diamonds mask-like around their eyes. Their noses were similar to an ant-eater's, only these were bent like accordions. They stepped further into the clearing, and I saw they were the size of coyotes. The black markings continued up their back and down their tails, which were corkscrew-shaped—a sudden, uneasy reminder of my frightful experience in the professor's barn.

"What are they?" I asked.

"Toves," Amabelle said.

"They're a little *strange* looking."

"They are *slithy* looking," she corrected.

One tove stuck its nose in a broken piece of pottery and gave it a sniff. The other began rolling around the hollowed dirt at the sundial's base; the wabe.

Amabelle laughed.

"What's it doing?"

"Gyring and gimbling!"

"What does that mean?"

"What it is doing."

"I see," I said.

The one not gyring and gimbling made a series of three honking sounds, each a different pitch. It paused and repeated the sounds exactly.

I mimicked them. Immediately the creature jolted and stared at me.

"You sound just like them!" Amabelle said. "Do it again!"

So I did.

The tove lumbered over to me. I pulled my legs onto the stump, crossing them when it got close.

"They will not hurt you," Amabelle said. "Here." She fed the tove something from her pocket.

"What was that?"

"Cheese. Make the sound again."

I did, only louder. The other stopped rolling and came over for cheese. Within minutes, more bent snouts appeared from the woods. Soon, we found ourselves in the thick of a dozen toves.

"You can call them!" Amabelle shrieked.

"Apparently," I said, uneasily.

"Never have I seen so many at once. They are too fearful of le Bandersnatch."

"What's a Bandersnatch?"

"You never want to know," she said, seriously. "Usually by now they sleep. But if ever you see one, run! They are wicked and horrible."

To be honest, I didn't exactly find the toves cute and cuddly. I wasn't overly disappointed when we ran out of cheese and all but the original two lumbered back into the woods. The remaining ones nestled in the wabe of their respective sundials and slept. "How'll I know if I see one?"

"You will know." Amabelle's gaze fell to the swords in my lap. "Where did you get those?"

"I brought them from England. One used to be my brother Harry's. He died."

"Was he older or younger?"

"Older," I said. Then I realized something strange. "I nearly forgot. To-morrow is my birthday." Perhaps I'd forgotten on purpose. Until then, all my birthdays had been during happy times. This one wasn't.

My birthday turned out well. Surprisingly so.

Twice in the night, I awoke to father speaking of borogroves and slithy toves, but by morning his fever had fallen nearly three degrees. He had even become lucid enough for me to tell him about the professor and the vorpal creatures.

He sat up. "You must show me."

"No, the doctor said you needed rest."

"I'm feeling much better and, besides, a little exercise and fresh air might be good."

Grudgingly, I acquiesced and, along with Amabelle, brought him out to the garden. A new tree, as tall as any other in the woods, stood marking the trail entrance. It had bright yellow and blue leaves, and a lime colored trunk. Amabelle pressed her ear against it. "It's a Tumtum tree. Listen."

Father and I took turns listening. It sounded as if a bright timpani drum were being struck deep within. "Tum! Tum!"

It seemed to especially intrigue Father. Even after showing him three borogroves and a rath, he stopped to listen to the tree again on our way back to the house. "It's the most amazing thing I've ever heard," he said.

Father returned to bed. Amabelle had chores to do. I wandered the garden. Noticing the barn door again unlocked, I ventured another visit with the professor.

Surprisingly, it seemed he'd been expecting me. "Yesterday you so impressed me with your fine fencing, I made you a special gift."

I blushed. Amabelle must have told Mrs. Renoir about my birthday, who, in turn, must have told the professor.

In his hands rested an *actual* sword. Holding it carefully by the blade, he presented me with its hilt.

I gasped. "Truly? For me?"

"Truly."

Grasping the handle, I hefted it. It was heavy. "What's it made from? Is it real?"

He gestured with his palm. "As real as everything else. What is real and is not, eh? It is forged from bronze. Three thousand years ago, it would have been the most advanced weapon on the earth."

I swished it. It felt real. "It's absolutely perfect, Mr. . . . Professor. Thank you!"

"You may call me Professor Tesla," he said. "And I am happy you approve. Now you may continue your studies with a more authentic rapier."

The day after my birthday turned out bad again. I awoke to Father worse than ever.

"Today the professor went into town," Amabelle said. "*Ma mère* asked him to return with *le docteur*."

I wiped Father's face with the compress, but it had little effect. He was unconscious and back into high fever. As it was best to let him rest, I took my new bronze sword outside.

The weight of a real sword made thrusting and parrying much more difficult. Soon, my arm ached and I needed a break from my practice. It was then I noticed Professor Tesla had left the barn doors unlocked.

Filled with curiosity, I snuck inside, wanting to peek at his laboratory without him watching me. Above my head, the titanic ball and corkscrew loomed like sleeping giants. I discovered a cardboard cutout of a full-sized person glued to the back wall, probably traced from the professor's own body.

With a step back, I extended my blade to it. "*En garde!*" I parried, then came round with an outside swoop, quickly snapping my wrist into a block the way Harry used to. "Do you take me for a fool?" I asked it. Then, I brought the sword back over my head with both hands to land the final blow. "I'll teach you what we do with fools!"

Just as I swung the sword upward, a crack of electrostatic ripped the air apart. I realized too late the professor's machine had not been asleep at all. With a flash, lightning exploded up the corkscrew and flew through the ring, splitting into two long zigzagging bolts. One stretched to the sphere, dancing and tapping chaotically on its surface, the other pushed its blue white fingers into the tip of the blade I held straight up over my head. A blast of current sparked up and down my sword, tightening my grip. From the blade's center, a burst of white-hot light erupted. Screeching, searing static screamed in my ears. Ozone filled my senses.

I closed my eyes, expecting never to open them again.

My mind went blindingly white.

The white pulled into a thin horizontal line.

Then it was over.

The noise, the shocks, the static charges, all of it just died away. I lowered my arms and dropped the sword, flexing my fingers as it fell heavily onto the dirt floor. The ground violently shook. It was an earthquake!

Slamming my eyes closed, I braced, waiting for the apparatus above to tumble and crush me. But then, the tremor ended. I took a deep breath, picked up my sword, and decided to leave the barn before something else happened. Halfway to the door, I stopped.

I had noticed the sword in my hand. It now was suddenly completely different.

Longer, slender, more elegant—it had even changed color. The blade was now a polished cobalt, matching the squares suspended above me in a ring, and the hilt was a polished mirror that winked as I turned my wrist in the light. Discreetly, I smuggled the sword into the house and slid it beneath my bed.

When Professor Tesla finally returned to the house, the sun had already fallen. Two men, neither of them doctors, accompanied him. From my bedroom window, I secretly watched and listened to the three of them argue in French while they stood in front of the barn's doorway. One man anxiously spoke of an explosion ten kilometers away. The other kept marking a map and thrusting it into Professor Tesla's face. "Your fault!" he said repeatedly.

When the men finally left, Professor Tesla hung his head and stood in the shadow of his barn, the folded map clenched in his fingers. I crept into my bed, thinking about what had happened earlier. I had no doubts that I was responsible for this explosion, not Professor Tesla. Guilt ate away at me.

When I finally heard the wooden stairs squeak and the professor pull his bedroom door closed, I knew what I had to do.

I dressed, wet down Father's face one last time, and waited until Professor Tesla began snoring. Then I tip-toed across the hall and quietly opened his door. He continued to snore as I pinched the map from the table beside his bed.

A quarter moon and a velvet belt of stars filled the sky as I stole across the garden. With nary a glance be-hind, I slipped down the path and vanished into the shadows of the gloomy woods.

The map was not easy to follow, especially in the dark. In some places, the trees, roots, and branches grew so thick and tangled, it blocked almost all light from the night sky, forcing me to guess my way in the pitch black. Luckily, markers in the woods matched markers on the map. It would have been an impossible journey other-wise.

Knowing only that there was an explosion, I'm not sure what I expected to find at the end of my hunt. I suppose my conscience simply sought a path to retribu-tion. Certainly, guilt drove most of my actions. I kept thinking of Mum's letter, telling me how she knew I would make her proud, and that she would always be watching me. How proud was she right now?

What I utterly failed to consider was that it wasn't a *proper* explosion at all, but an explosion between reality and dreams that tore open a hole in the vorpal big enough for a nightmare to come through.

My mind was so caught up with guilt and Mum, I didn't even notice the shuddering cracks of trees falling until the forest snapped right in front of me, revealing the most gruesome creature my eyes ever beheld. It stood beneath the moon on two clawed feet, with scaly dragon skin the reddish purple hue of an aubergine. Antennae twisted from the top of its oval head. Fire burned in its evil eyes.

I stood frozen with fear as each of its claws grabbed onto a tree and it raised itself up, flexing the bat wings attached to its shoulder blades. It fully extended its snake-like neck until it was tall enough to see over the woods. Even from five stories beneath it, I saw the moonlight twinkle off the edge of its razor sharp teeth as its mouth opened and it bellowed something terrible and threatening into the night.

I did the only thing I could.

As fast as my feet would go, I ran, and ran, and ran.

My chest burned. The muscles in my legs wound up like springs. My stomach kept convulsing and cramping. Morning had broken by the time I finally burst from the woods into the garden of the house. The east edge of the sky glowed pink as, coughing, I ran for the backdoor, nearly failing to notice the barn.

The doors had been thrown open, the chain busted. The barn completely empty. Everything was gone. Not a trace of any of the apparatus remained, just a hard packed dirt floor in an old wooden structure that time was slowly pulling to pieces.

I found Mrs. Renoir sobbing hysterically at the kitchen table. She began sputtering to me in French, too quickly for me to understand. Amabelle ran in. "They took him away!" she said. "And his things. Three carriages."

"Who?" I asked. "*Who* took him?"

"Men in black coats. They spoke a different language."

"Did they hurt him? What did he say?"

Her gaze dropped to the floor. "He said not a thing to us. He looked sad."

I pushed back my hair, trying to make sense of things. Who would take the professor? Were they violent? Did this have anything to do with the monster in the woods? The monster that only a *vorpal* weapon could stop?

"I . . . I have to go!" I rushed upstairs. My father was asleep as I dropped beside the bed to retrieve my sword. Suddenly, his eyes snapped open, giving me a fright. They were blue and wild. "Beware the Jabberwock, my son!" he said. "The jaws that bite, the claws that catch! Beware the Jubjub bird, and shun the frumious Bandersnatch!"

I understood the jaws and claws. Plunging the rag into the bucket, I dabbed his face furiously, and nodded. "I will Father. I will." This calmed him and he closed his eyes again. I kissed his forehead. Sliding my sword out from under the bed, I hefted it and went back to face the Jabberwock.

The return trip took even longer. Exhaustion was taking its toll and threatened to destroy me before I even reached the Jabberwock. So, once I was close, I stopped to rest beneath a clutch of Tumtum trees. Their timpanis tummed as I thought of facing the malicious beast I had witnessed standing taller than the treetops with claws ending in steely knives, and a mouth full of razor-sharpened teeth.

As my strength returned, my bravery faltered. Each passing second took a piece of my confidence. Time was turning me into a coward. This battle could easily become my end.

Fear poured into me.

Nearby, a twig snapped, yanking me out of the waist-deep slough of insecurity in which I'd been wading. Clamoring to my feet, I listened hard. Another snap, this one even closer. I turned, holding my sword at the ready, waiting to plunge my blade straight into the thing as it came through the trees.

So fixed on destroying the Jabberwock was I that I barely managed to hold back my thrust when, at the last possible moment, I saw that it was Amabelle.

"What are you doing?" I asked in an out-of-breath fearful rage. "I almost killed you!"

"I came after you," she said. "You seemed upset."

"You have to go back home. Now!"

She crossed her arms. "No!"

"Yes! You must! You don't understand! There's . . . "

But it was too late. The Jabberwock's approach thundered through the trees. It was coming fast, a stream of ugly sounds burbling from its venomous mouth. Amabelle's eyes became saucers. "What is that?"

I stepped in front of her, facing the monster's approach. "The Jabberwock."

The ground shook from the toppling of trees. With a loud crack, the forest in front of us snapped like twigs. I barely pulled Amabelle out of the way as they crashed down all around us.

Amabelle's face drained of color. Her mouth opened, but her scream caught in her throat, unable to make it to her lips.

Tightening my grip on my vorpal sword, I heaved my blade, ready to swing.

With a sweep of its claw, the Jabberwock flicked me aside, slamming me hard into a tree, knocking the wind from my lungs. My sword spun from my hand. When I could breathe again, I turned to retrieve it. But I stopped when I saw something—yet *another* thing—standing in the way.

As Amabelle had promised, I knew what it was the moment I laid my eyes upon it. It was a Bandersnatch: a lizard with a serpentine neck, and a head composed entirely of a shark's mouth full of double razor teeth. The teeth snapped frumiously as the neck lunged them toward me. I dove out of the way, landing in a twist of brambles, ripping my arm open on thorns.

Amabelle's scream found her mouth as the Jabberwock wheeled on her.

I freed myself from the brambles, and the Bandersnatch curved its neck and went for me again. I somersaulted over it, smelling the foul stench of its breath as I grazed the top of its mandibles.

That was too close. I couldn't keep this up.

My mind raced for a way to get at my sword. The only advice Amabelle had ever offered me on

Bandersnatches was to hide from them. That wasn't very useful. I had to face it, not hide away like a tove.

Wait, *the toves!* An idea flashed in my mind.

The Bandersnatch recoiled, readying for another attack. I had nowhere to go, or anytime to get there. Either my idea would work, or in the next instant I would be torn to shreds.

Cupping my hands around my mouth, I hollered my mimic of the three note tove call as loud as I could. It echoed through the woods, seeming to come back from every direction.

My tactic worked. The creature hesitated, quickly snapping its neck around so the teeth faced behind it. I made the call again. Still snapping crazily at the empty trees in search of toves, it slowly turned its reptilian body to face the same direction as its teeth.

I continued to make the call, and the Bandersnatch slowly plodded forward, walking atop of my vorpal sword. The instant its back foot came off my blade, I snatched the sword up and, with one *snicker-snack!* swoop, I chopped the Bandersnatch's head clean off at the neck.

From behind me, Amabelle screamed.

She was clutched in the Jabberwock's monstrous claw as it lifted her toward its rapacious mouth.

I scrambled for the beast and leapt up onto its tail. Trying to wrap my arm around it, I found its girth far too great, and I began slipping down. I brought the fingers of my free hand back around, and clutched one of the spiny bumps that ran up the center of the Jabberwock's backside. The tail whipped angrily back and forth. I pulled myself up, wrapped my legs around the tail, squeezing just below my handhold. Then I let go and reached forward, pulling myself higher.

In this manner, I was able to get to the top of the tail, just before the Jabberwock prepared to stuff Amabelle into its mouth. It held her there, locked in its claws, and, curious about me, curved its neck back see what I was up to. With my legs wrapped tightly around the creature, I held my sword over my head.

With all my might, I plunged the blade into its hide.

The woods filled with a deafening howl. The monster's neck extended as it threw back its head.

But Amabelle remained trapped in its claws.

I climbed onto the hilt of my sword and grabbed the creature's spine farther up. With some strain, I pulled my blade free. The Jabberwock's head charged back around quickly, those teeth constantly snapping.

Using my hand as a fulcrum, I swung over the other way and stuck my sword higher into the side of its back.

Again it bellowed in pain. Again I struggled to make my way upward. And still sweet Amabelle remained in its grasp.

The Jabberwock didn't fall for my move a fourth time. It came one way, gnashing its teeth, and then, just as I was ready to swing at its neck, it suddenly came round the other way. It happened so quickly, I barely managed to dodge its fangs. In the last instance, I leapt up as high as I could, clutching its bumpy carapace with one hand as my other drove my blade as deeply as it could straight into the monster's back, separating sections of its spine.

This brought a thundering wail of agony from the Jabberwock that shook the ground around us.

Now I was high enough to use the hilt of my sword as a step up to the valley between the demon's shoulder blades where its leathery bat wings met in a *V* formation. Once in position, I reached down and pulled out my sword.

What luck! I had actually found a position on its backside where I was safe from its teeth. Its neck flipped and whipped wildly as it gnashed the air around me, trying to snap me in its jaws. Through this, I would catch brief glimpses of Amabelle, terrified.

Kneeling up in the black rise of its wings, I hoisted my sword over my shoulder, and, with one solid slice, cut right through the Jabberwock's neck with a loud *snicker-snack!*

Its oval mouth slowly opened wide revealing all its razor teeth, but no sound came out. The snapping and twisting stopped, and time seemed to slow as the head fell to the ground with a dead thump. Black blood oozed like tar from its open neck. Its claws fell limply open as the rest of the body slowly tumbled forward.

"Jump!" I yelled to Amabelle.

She did, landing in a whortleberry bush barely out of harm's way, while I, with my sword at my side, rode hundreds of stones of meat all the way to the ground.

"Are you all right?" I called out to Amabelle.

"Is it over?" asked the whortleberry bush, some of the ripe black-hearts falling from its vine as it shook. "Can we go home?"

"Yes." I kicked the side of the Jabberwock's head. "But this is coming with us."

It took most of the day for us to make it back. Amabelle did not possess my stamina for walking, especially with the added burden of having to assist me in carrying the Jabberwock's head.

"It is an ugly thing," she kept saying. "Why do you want to bring it to *ma mère*? She will not be happy."

But I insisted.

By lunch time, Amabelle no longer complained about the head as much as she did about being hungry. As fortune would have it, thirst wasn't a problem; the forest was full of brooks babbling with cold water running down from the melting northern ice caps.

We stopped four times to drink, resting a while each time. Twice, inquisitive borogroves came out of the woods to greet us and sniff the Jabberwock's head. I had to shoo one away when it turned and lifted its leg to relieve itself on it.

"See?" Amabelle said. "Even *they* think it is ugly."

Mrs. Renoir was beside herself with worry when we reached the house. She hugged her daughter then chided her about running off without telling anyone. I had trouble following her French but when she finished, Amabelle said to me, "*Ma mère* says if not that you were missing too she would have died of fear, but she knew you would look after me."

I was glad we had left the Jabberwock's head outside and Mrs. Renoir didn't yet know the perils I had submitted her daughter to. I smiled, but a grave look fell over Mrs. Renoir's face when she returned my glance. "*Votre père . . .*" she started.

I didn't need to hear the rest. I scurried upstairs to our room to find Father worse than ever. I pressed the wet cloth to his face. His skin burned to the touch. Amabelle came in behind me. "*Ma mère* says *le docteur* is coming soon."

Father moaned. His blue eyes opened with watery comprehension and he spoke, his voice barely above a whisper. I lowered my ear to his lips. "And hast thou slain the Jabberwock?"

I nodded. "Yes, Father."

Pride washed over him, and, even in his sick state, he managed a smile. "Come to my arms, my beamish boy!" he rasped, and with great effort raised his arms to my shoulders. "O frabjous day! Callooh! Callay!" I had never seen him so happy or so proud.

He died that way.

Tears came to my eyes as I stood over him. Gently, I closed his eyelids and sobbed. I had nobody left. Time had taken my mother, my older brother, and now my father.

I felt Amabelle's small hand creep into mine. She said not a word, just stood beside me, holding my hand, sharing my tears. A long time passed until I was ready to leave that room, and she stayed there with me.

For that, I am eternally grateful.

We buried my father the next day at the foot of the Tumtum tree at the edge of the woods, covering the grave with a small pile of white stones. On the tree above, I hung a sign I made, using my vorpal sword to carve out the words. It read: *Here lies Giles Harry Covington. May he find in death some of the adventure he longed for in life.*

It truly is my hope that he did.

Without the professor, Mrs. Renoir would have been unable to continue running *Le Petit Lapin* if it weren't for the sudden influx of tourism generated by the news of the fascinating creatures living in the woods around the house. It became one of the top places in France to vacation, attracting people from all across Europe. Even the Welsh journalist Sir Henry Morton Stanley spent four nights in the care of Mrs. Renoir on his way back to London after successfully locating Dr. Livingstone .

I stayed on with Mrs. Renoir until Amabelle became a proper young lady. Then, at the tender age of eighteen, I asked for her hand in marriage, and, to my delight, she gave it. We decided to move back to England, where we found a quaint cottage nestled in the town of Abington, just south of Oxford and west of the river Isis.

We return for a fortnight stay with Amabelle's mum every six months, and, although it's been years since nary a borogrove or a rath or a tove or even a Bandersnatch has been spotted anywhere in France, *Le Petit Lapin's* business continues to thrive. Mostly it's from that year following Professor Tesla's disappearance. So many people stayed at the house during that time, Mrs. Renoir's reputation for good food and impeccable service made its way around the world and back. But it's partly due to the head still mounted above the two-story brick fireplace on the northern wall of the drawing room.

Guests sit beneath its looming shadow, in comfortable chairs and worn sofas, and they read their papers, and drink their tea, and play games of backgammon, occasionally stopping to give it a look.

Like everything, it has paid a toll to time. These days, its twisted antennae—so long they touch the ceiling—look more like dead branches. Its hollow eyes that once burned red fire, have now faded to dull pink. The tendrils on either side of its mouth hang limply straight toward the floor like the moustache of a lower caste Spaniard. But people still see that oval mouth locked in its toothy sneer, and they talk about the way it whiffled and burbled as it came through the tulgey woods, and how things might have been if it weren't for the vorpal sword hanging proudly below it.

Then they go back to their papers, and their tea, and their backgammon, and think about their future.

I am one of them as I write this story, seated in the oldest of the two sofas near the back of the room—the only piece of furniture still surviving from when Father and I arrived at *Le Petit Lapin* that summer evening so many years ago. Amabelle is beside me, reading a copy of *Harper's* and sipping her tea. For her, time is still giving. She notices me looking and smiles, and, even though the freckles faded years ago, I can still see that little girl in the dirty pinafore clapping her hands and laughing at the mimsy borogrove being tripped up by the mome raths.

Her skin is radiant. Her hair is shorter than when she was a girl but still soft and chestnut. I look down at her belly, much larger than ever due to the baby that has been growing inside for the past eight months.

After all this writing, I realize I am the same as the people glancing up at the head of the Jabberwock. I've said everything there is to say. I have thought enough about it. All that has happened, all that could have happened.

This story is finished.

Now we live the next.

I wrote this story three times. Each time, it became more and more like a story poem of the type Neil Gaiman writes. I am rather fond of it in its present form.

I will say it kept me up an entire night working on it. I think I wrote nonstop for almost sixteen hours before finally coming away with what was finally the piece I was looking for.

And by then, I had the perfect dedication for it, to my daughter:

For Valentine:

> *whose central incisors were accidentally removed*
> *by her brother **three** years ahead of schedule.*

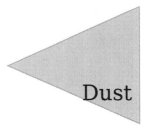

Dust

Asoft spattering of notes; piano strings plucked with the hammers held back. A frozen breath. A crystal cloud. And, appearing in the center, Juniper Brandywine.

Her pink teardrop slippers sink into the thick hand-knitted comfort warming five-year-old Emily Spears whose face is so close, the wind from her lips flutters Junipers wings. No longer a nuisance, time has promoted Emily to Scourge, to Bane, Opponent, Nemesis . . .

And soon, Juniper thinks, *Assassin.* She shivers, equal parts fear and withdrawal.

Emily giggles. The vacuity between her Lateral Incisors grips Juniper's attention. *Nonstop service straight to Hell's kitchen.* Emily's brother's boot unintentionally opened the milk tooth passage seventeen days ago (Christopher Spears, age thirteen, fully vested last Christmas).

Emily drones. Garbled nonsense, to Juniper, anyway. Prosaic banality without redemption. Just . . . grey.

Then Emily laughs. An empty laugh. But Juniper seizes the opportunity to make a hopeful appraisal.

Alas, her heart sinks. Random chance extracted Emily's Central Incisors early. Months wait for her others.

With a sigh, Juniper unties a purple sack from her belt.   Inside,   no   surprise; a day, maybe two, and Juniper dies.

She wretches and wobbles. Shaking, convulsing, she licks and dips her fingertip into the bag. It comes out sparkling.

Dust

Juniper snorts most and licks the rest. Remembering young, naïve days with her friends; her clique; her cabal; her camarilla. They were invincible, flying through the Hollow and laughing at Faders both secretly and openly.

Faders had no excuses, with such work aplenty and a market growing bullish faster than inflation in Emily's world. At least no excuses that mattered. Two bits, three bits, even ten-dollar checks Juniper would happily sign. Baby teeth brought a hundred times more, even unrefined. And turned into Pixie Dust? Triple that value again.

No excuses in this economy, Juniper thought. Well, at least she did back then.

Her blood saturates and Juniper's legs stabilize, making her *feel* normal again, but she's marked and constantly reminded she's not normal by her faded skin. Four fixes left she estimates and reties the bag to her waist.

She sings. Her voice, unlike her body, still perfect; blue bells and glass bottles; waves, wind and wooden chimes. Although much falls beyond human ears, and Emily cannot understand the tongue, the child's eyes grow heavy, until quiet snores blow back Juniper's wings.

Hopefully, Emily sleeps till daybreak; a wish Juniper knows futile, for tomorrow when Emily summons, Juniper will die.

She needs something she stopped believing in seventeen days ago, when she came to harvest Emily's Central Incisors one year ahead of schedule.

Easy work. Standard operation.

Take two teeth, leave four quarters.

Piece of cake.

Admittedly, Juniper had limited experience in multi-tooth transactions, and this doubled her standard currency load, but she wasn't worried. She had tenure. Years of service without a single problem on the books.

She appeared after midnight, easily procuring each tooth without even needing to enlist the help of her Pillow Jack.

Quarters one and two slipped under the case, quietly and quickly. Three required more force, but it went. Oh, how she wishes she'd stopped at seventy-five cents. How different her life would be.

And longer, she adds.

But she didn't stop.

And the fourth quarter

got jammed.

Juniper pushed. She prodded. She kicked and she cussed. And then, Emily Spears, aged five-and=three-quarters, Human child, woke up.

Juniper panicked. *What if she screams? What is she cries?* Juniper took stock, and a deep breath. With two Central Incisors securely tethered to her belt, and four quarters in place (more or less), and half a bag of Pixie Dust, there was no reason for pause. Yet she kept a hand in her pouch for a quick getaway, in case she was wrong.

But Juniper heard nothing from Emily. No screams, no cries. Only saw wonder and awe in the child's eyes. And for once in her life, Juniper felt affection toward a Human (An attraction she would later blame for impairing her judgment).

Touching the child's warm cheek, she said, "You're a cutie-pie," and Emily smiled. Then, with a voice unmatched by a thousand-angel choir, Juniper sang to the girl:

Sleep a sweet sleep
Dream a sweet dream
We'll dance through the meadow
And hide in the trees

From the top of the staircase
To the dimples on your face
Treetop to root stem
One two three and back again
Your world to my world
My time to your time

A gift for small Emily
With love
From Juniper Brandywine

Of course, Emily understood none of the words. Juniper had expected the girl to fall back to sleep, but she hadn't. Instead, she giggled and babbled in monotone grey; ugly sounds, like the ones always coming from Emily's species, reminding Juniper of factories, pollution, and death; wrecking the moment—leaving Juniper feeling awkward, uncomfortable, and wanting to leave.

Filling her palm with Dust from her pouch, Juniper gave a wave before disappearing into an eddy of sparkling mist. At least, that was the plan. Only, she never got quite that far, because something happened. Something that, to Juniper's knowledge, hadn't happened for hundreds of years.

Something impossible.

The girl made more noise, lying there in bed. Only this time, Juniper understood the two words Emily said. Real words. Not perfect, not poetic, not wrapped the way Juniper's mother had intended in beautiful, melodic phrase. But words, very real. *Very* real, just the same.

And when Emily Spears said, "Juniper Brandywine," Juniper swallowed hard. She understood this time.

From the lips of a Human (a child no less), came Juniper's *real* Faerie name. And instantly, the two were bound together; Juniper as slave and servant, to be summoned at the fancy of master Emily, Human child, aged five-and-three-quarters.

After that, whenever she woke, Emily called the name. And Juniper would come sing her to sleep, four times a night or more. Exhausted, Juniper found her work beginning to suffer—she couldn't harvest fast enough to keep up with the Pixie Dust. She didn't eat. She didn't sleep. She became paranoid, never knowing when she'd be snatched from the Hollow and made to perform again.

The following week, Juniper noticed a change. First on her breasts and tummy, then on her legs and arms. Soon she couldn't hide it when she went out in public. Other Faeries shunned her. Her friends taunted her. Her camarilla teased her, called her Fader.

And she was.

Tonight, finally, Emily's again asleep. Hoping it lasts till sunrise, Juniper sniffles, and wipes a tear from her cheek. From her pouch she extracts just enough Dust to return home for one last day in the Hollow.

How shall she spend it? Alone? Walking through the gardens? Reading by the riverbank?

Her body quivers uncontrollably, coming down off the Dust, and she thinks, *The point is moot.* Tomorrow will be spent in cold sweats, wrapped in the fetal position, holding back vomit.

Threatening to steal even this, Emily opens her mouth and yawns, giving Juniper one last tease of perfect baby teeth before going back to sleep.

Oh, if only she would lose another before Juniper's time ends. But it would take a miracle, and Juniper no longer believes in them.

Of course, it's *possible*, in *theory*. Just, very unlikely. But, Christopher *could* boot her again. Emily *could* fall down the stairs. A baseball *could* slam into the side of her head.

Oh, who is Juniper kidding with all this wishful thinking?

Releasing her handful of Pixie Dust envelops her in swirling stars and Juniper takes her last voyage home, unsure of how she feels. Afraid. Sad. Angry.

But mainly, just empty and alone.

Until—

Watching the image of Emily fade, Juniper gets

An

Idea.

The next night, Emily calls much later than her usual time. So late, Juniper had given up hope of doing anything but dying.

She spent the day rationing Pixie Dust. Not that it mattered. There wasn't nearly enough to stop her shaking or vomiting. But Juniper worked through it, scheming, outfitting, mentally preparing, and talking herself back every time she second-guessed the whole crazy, harebrained plan she had built in her mind.

And it *was* crazy, going against everything she knew. Yet, there was no other way. Desperate times called for desperate measures. Survival of the fittest. Glass half full and all of that.

Juniper knew, though, that the truth wasn't nearly so romantic. The force guiding her actions had far more to do with needing another fix of Dust. Still, the platitudes helped. Besides, in the end, did why matter much?

Ready by nine, Emily time, Juniper waited for the call.

And waited.

And waited.

Ten o'clock came and she vomited.

And waited.

At midnight, she finished the Pixie Dust and vomited some more.

And at one, she finished it again, turning the bag inside out, licking the fabric to get every speck. Then, with blurry vision and blood-laced bile and no color left in her skin,

Juniper began

To wither.

Thirty minutes later, her Faerie name issued from Emily's head, ripping Juniper out of the Hollow, shaking, sweating, dizzy, disoriented, and into Emily's bed.

Her eyes thick with sleep, Emily watches the twinkling colors. She thinks of glass slippers, pumpkin coaches, and Fairy Godmothers. Her new dolly will appear from the fire and the chimes and sing her back to sleep.

Juniper Brandywine.

The best gift the Tooth Fairy ever gave anyone, Emily suspects. She has lots more teeth; she hopes for lots more magical fairy dolls.

In the cloud is a familiar silhouette: butterfly wings, velvet dress, golden belt of twine. Emily's most precious gift.

Juniper Brandywine.

Through a yawn, Emily smiles. She rubs her eyes and refocuses. Juniper seems different tonight: unhappy, and her skin is white. And she smells funny. And she isn't glowing like she normally does, making Emily squint to see what Juniper holds in her hands. It runs down between her feet. Too dark to make out details, Emily moves closer again.

Juniper strains to lift the thing up. It looks heavy, but she gets it over her head. Emily peers just inches away, squeezing her eyes practically closed, until finally she recognizes what juniper holds.

A sledgehammer. Like the one Emily's Dad used to drive in fence posts last summer.

None of Emily's other dolls ever came with this accessory. Wondering why Juniper has, she opens her mouth to query.

A blur. A crack. Just one swing to her head. And Juniper knocks every tooth out of Emily's mouth, showering them onto the bed.

Emily screams, her tender throat filling up with blood.

Juniper finds a place to hide when Emily's parents come. They seem confused. *What's wrong, Emily?* They ask, frantically glancing around the room. *You must have fallen out of bed. Or something.*

They rush her off to the hospital and Juniper puts one of the teeth under Emily's pillow.

And waits.

And waits.

She vomits on Emily's sheets.

And waits.

Rainbow Icefrost, with two quarters, eventually shows up to harvest the tooth. Juniper surprises her and negotiations then ensue. Trading Rainbow a second tooth for a gram of Pixie Dust, Juniper fixes.

She steals the fifty cents Rainbow leaves under Emily's pillow before going back to the Hollow.

The doctor at the hospital seems confused and decides Emily's parents are right: *She must have fallen out of bed. Or something.*

Later in Emily's room, Mom is slightly troubled when she can't find her daughter's missing teeth. *Don't worry*, she says, *the Tooth Fairy will come anyway.* And leaves her with a goodnight kiss.

It only makes Emily feel worse, staring at her ceiling, terrified that the Tooth Fairy *will* come and unleash another magic fairy doll. Only this time accessorized with a cheese grater. Or a blowtorch. Or a shotgun.

Or a chainsaw.

Emily gets little sleep that night or the next. The entire month, in fact, brings hardly any rest. Every single doll she owns gets tossed into the trash. She can't eat solid foods for almost a year and a half.

And every day after that, the rest of her long life . . .

Not once,

Not one single time,

Does Emily ever utter the name

Of Juniper Brandywine.

I go to meditation class once a week, and the Buddhist monk giving the meditations always tells a story between them. One particular night, he described what it would be like to meet a real Buddha and how you probably wouldn't even know it at first—you'd only start to notice little things about him that were different from everyone else. Like, how, wherever he went, he brought peace and happiness. And how people were oddly attracted to him. He would help others without them directly knowing they were being helped.

Well I came out of meditation that night with not only a peaceful mind, but also with this novella which has enough sentiment it actually made my mother cry.

Angels

1

No fair!" Annabelle Parks shouted as she toppled sideways. Jamie-Lynn had just hit her in the side of the head with a pillow. Annabelle hadn't been ready. She sat back up in her sleeping bag, her long thin hair a mass of tangled blonde.

"Everything's fair. All rules are on," Jamie-Lynn Howard said. She had no idea what it meant, but it was something they both always said. Usually after one of them shouted, "No fair!"

"Okay you guys, calm down," Jamie-Lynn's dad said, coming into the room with a platter of sandwiches.

He set the platter down on the coffee table. The girls were having a sleepover at Jamie-Lynn's house, the way they often did. Jamie-Lynn's mom was currently over at Annabelle's for her weekly game of Texas Hold'em. Jamie-Lynn's dad hated games, and he hated card games the most, he often said. So he generally supervised the sleepovers—at least until Jamie-Lynn's mom got home. By then, the girls were supposed to be asleep. They never were, though. Truth was, during the sleepover nights at Jamie-Lynn's house, the girls rarely got much sleep at all. But nobody cared much about that. Not really.

"Thanks dad!" Jamie-Lynn said.

"Thanks, Mr. H!" Annabelle said.

"At your service," Jamie-Lynn's dad said with a humble bow. He had brown eyes and brown hair, both almost exactly the same color as Jamie Lynn's, only Jamie Lynn's hair hung down to her shoulders, whereas her dad's hair was cut very short.

"How's the movie?" he asked. "Enough blood for you?"

"It's awesome!" Annabelle said.

"You wouldn't even know!" Jamie-Lynn said, and then to her dad added, "She hides under the blankets every time the music gets even a little scary."

"Wanna know a secret Annabelle?" Jamie-Lynn's dad whispered. "I would too." He turned to leave. "Well you guys, enjoy. I have to go make sure Ryan is okay."

Ryan was Jamie-Lynn's younger brother. He was ten years old, and was born with cystic fibrosis. Currently, he was having a pretty bad attack and had missed the last few days of school, bed-ridden. The only time he got to go anywhere at all was to see the doctor.

"I'll come down and check on you again in a bit," said Jamie-Lynn's dad before disappearing back upstairs.

Jamie-Lynn didn't always get along so well with her dad, but on sleepover nights, things were different. On sleepover nights, *he* was different. Maybe it was because her mom wasn't home. Or maybe he was just showing off because Annabelle was over. Whatever the reason, he was somehow more tolerable.

The sandwiches were cut into quarters and were of three varieties: peanut butter and jelly, devilled egg, and cheese and pickles. The girls always slept in the living room during their sleepovers, and they always rearranged things the same way: first they pushed the coffee table way back so it butted up against the front of the sofa, giving them ample room to lay out their sleeping bags in front of the TV. Then they plopped their pillows down. The next step was to slide the first movie into the DVD player. They always watched three movies, and usually the movies all fit into a theme.

Tonight was horror night, and the movies were all senseless slasher types with chainsaws and butcher knives and endless blood splatter. Both girls had a half-finished bowl of popcorn beside their pillows. The popcorn had been the first course Jamie-Lynn's dad had brought down. The sandwiches were the second. Usually he brought them at least three different courses of food throughout the evening.

"You're dad's pretty cool," Annabelle said, taking a peanut butter and jelly sandwich off the tray. "I wish my dad was as cool as yours." Unlike Jamie-Lynn, Annabelle's parents were split up. She lived with her mom most of the time, and saw her dad on holidays and the occasional weekend.

"My dad's not that cool," Jamie-Lynn said. "You just like him because he brings you food." She slammed Annabelle in the side of the head with her pillow again.

Annabelle tumbled, sandwich and all. "Hey! No fair! I'm eating!"

"Everything's fair. All rules are on."

Just then, from the television behind them, the music grew in tension and came to a crescendo that ended with the shrill sound of a woman screaming.

Annabelle jumped. Jamie-Lynn laughed.

"Maybe we should've picked different movies," Annabelle said.

"Aw, are you afraid?" Jamie-Lynn asked. "Gonna have nightmares? What are you, *twelve*?" In actual fact, both girls were fourteen. They both went to the same school, and were in the same seventh grade class. They had been best friends since kindergarten, and Jamie-Lynn's mom had been friends with Annabelle's mom for just as long.

Jamie-Lynn and Annabelle did everything together. They spent their lunch hours together, spent their recesses together, and had weekly sleepovers together. They shopped together, they ate together, they played together, they did school work together, and sometimes- —like tonight—they watched movies together.

But tonight was the first time Jamie-Lynn's dad had allowed the girls to watch these particular *types* of movies. He had finally decided they were old enough to understand the difference between *real* violence and *movie* violence. The DVDs the girls picked out from Jamie-Lynn's dad's collection were of the especially gruesome kind with axe wielding maniacs chasing college kids and chopping up their bodies before stuffing the parts into garbage bags. That sort of thing. When Jamie-Lynn's mom voiced her objection to their choices, her dad pointed out that these were *especially* harmless because they were so ridiculous they were actually more funny than scary. Jamie-Lynn's mom finally gave in, and so the girls got to watch their blood and gore.

It was all so exciting until they put one on.

Then the girls realized the movies were actually frightening.

Only Jamie-Lynn refused to admit she was in any way scared.

Had the girls known the movies were going to be so terrifying, they would probably have chosen them anyway because the fact was they didn't pick them because they wanted to see them so much as because they were finally *allowed* to. It was like being admitted into some secret club.

"I just don't think we need to subject ourselves to all this senseless violence, that's all," Annabelle said.

"Sure, that's what it is," Jamie-Lynn said.

"It is."

Another scream and Annabelle jumped again. Jamie-Lynn laughed even harder than before. "You're hilarious," she said.

"Thought your dad said these are so ridiculous they're funny," Annabelle said.

"He did."

"I don't find them funny at all."

Another scream. This time, both girls jumped and looked quickly away from the screen as an axe swung from above. Jamie-Lynn shuddered.

"Okay," Annabelle said, "how about we look through Ryan's DVDs? Maybe he's got *Beauty and the Beast* or something?"

That was a Friday night.

Even with the super scary movies, it was a good night and, as usual, both girls had a great time. When they woke up in the morning, Jamie-Lynn's dad made them French toast before driving Annabelle home (Annabelle lived five and a half miles from Jamie-Lynn—which was why Jamie-Lynn could walk to school and Annabelle had to take the bus). On Sunday, Jamie-Lynn saw Annabelle again, but only for a few hours. They went to the Northbridge Mall across town because Annabelle needed a new pair of sneakers. Her mom dropped them off and picked them up. She even gave them money for lunch at Burger King.

All in all, the whole weekend was pretty good. Jamie-Lynn went to bed on Sunday night thinking that it was nice having a best friend like Annabelle in her life— someone she could share things with, even if she never did tell Annabelle the truth about Friday: that those three movies had scared her just as much as they had scared Annabelle. Maybe even more so. Especially the last one. It was terrifyingly scary. She'd just hid the fact that she was frightened by poking fun at Annabelle being scared. Hiding her emotions was something Jamie-Lynn was good at.

But even though they'd both been scared neither girl ever had nightmares because of what they saw.

Not Friday night, not Saturday night, not Sunday night. In fact, Sunday night, Jamie-Lynn had particularly good dreams.

But then came Monday.

And that Monday turned out to be The Most Horrible of All Days.

2

When you dive off a high diving board, there's that split second before you hit the water when you realize your entire environment is about to change. Your brain suddenly understands you're about to go from a breathable air environment to an underwater environment where everything's different. In that same split second, you know you're about to feel your body parts slice into the water and everything—the temperature, your weight, even the pressure—will be completely different. You won't even be able to breathe. In that split second, if the board is high enough, you have time for second thoughts. It's in that split second when you think, *What if this hurts?*

A lot happens in that split second. It's also the point when your breath catches; when you brace; when you close your eyes and realize there's no way out. In that split second, you give in to the inevitable.

At 8:15 A.M. Monday morning, Annabelle was on her way to school wearing the new sneakers she'd bought at Northbridge Mall right before her and Jamie-Lynn went to Burger King. She had her pink backpack stuffed between her legs on the bus's floor. Annabelle had two backpacks she used for school interchangeably. One was pink, the other was blue with big yellow daisies on it. Jamie-Lynn only knew which backpack Annabelle had with her because she overheard Annabelle's mom talking to someone later about it. Jamie-Lynn knew the backpack was stuffed between Annabelle's legs, because that was how Annabelle always had it on the bus. Jamie-Lynn could have guessed the part about her wearing the new sneakers (because she had liked them so much when they found them in Target that she couldn't see her not wearing them to school), but she knew for sure because she overheard someone telling Principal Ryan outside the school after the assembly on Monday about seeing them on Annabelle's body after it was fished out of the Moonfalls River.

And she knew the time was 8:15 A.M., because *everybody* knew the time. 8:15 A.M. was the minute before it happened. The minute before Monday clicked over to 8:16 A.M. and became The Most Horrible of All Days. The minute before the school bus collided with an oncoming eighteen-wheeler truck and somehow went over onto the concrete edge of the Moonfalls River Bridge, levering up onto two of its wheels.

For a heartbeat, the way Jamie-Lynn saw it in her head, it sat balanced like that: up on two wheels, trying to decide which way to fall. It could go back down onto the bridge deck the way it came, or it could go the other way, over the side of the bridge. In Jamie-Lynn's mind that heartbeat seemed like an eternity as the bus sat suspended while God flipped a coin.

The coin slowly flipped, edge over edge, until coming down on the back of his hand.

Tails.

The bus quit balancing and gently tipped sideways, crashing through the bridge railing and tumbling down into the river.

The bus driver was the only survivor.

He somehow managed to undo his seatbelt, open the bus door, and swim up to safety without a scratch. In the coming days, he would be interviewed by all the local television news shows. Jamie-Lynn would PVR every interview. She would watch them, and re-watch them, and he would talk about how much grief, remorse, and regret he had over not being able to save a single kid on that bus.

Jamie-Lynn wouldn't buy it. She didn't think he'd even tried.

He came out of it too easy. If he *had* tried, he'd show signs of trying. Of course, he *claimed* to have tried. But, he said, the kids were panicking, kicking, screaming. He said the bus filled with water too fast. Jamie-Lynn thought it filled with water too fast because he opened the door so he could swim out to safety after getting his seat belt off. He said the kids all gathered to the back of the bus instead of the front. They were too far away for him to get to them. He said that if he'd gone for any of them, he'd just be dead too.

Jamie-Lynn thought he was a coward.

She wondered how much the driver contributed to the bus going off the bridge in the first place. Couldn't he have pulled it in a different direction? Couldn't he have done anything different? The part of Jamie-Lynn that actually believed Annabelle was dead needed to blame someone for what happened.

So she blamed that bus driver.

But mostly Jamie-Lynn had problems accepting Annabelle was gone. Even after hearing the news Monday morning, she kept expecting to see her at school or later outside with her new sneakers on her feet and her pink backpack strapped to her back, complaining about how the bus driver was an idiot, and that's why she was so late.

Jamie-Lynn even knew what seat Annabelle had been sitting in. She knew this because Annabelle always sat in the same one. Eight rows back on the right side— same side as the door. Probably less than fifteen feet away from it. Annabelle could swim. She was on the swim *team*. She was especially good at diving.

Annabelle knew about that last split second when you catch your breath and brace.

It made no sense.

It wasn't fair.

Everything's fair. All rules are on.

Except it wasn't. And they weren't.

The rules had all changed.

Sometime before nine that morning, once the school found out what had happened, there was a rally in the gymnasium where the kids were told. Everyone observed a moment of silence. Jamie-Lynn thought Annabelle deserved more than a moment.

After the rally, everyone was sent home for the rest of the day. Some kids seemed happy, like it was a surprise holiday.

Jamie-Lynn hated them almost as much as she would end up despising that bus driver.

3

"Honey, dinner's ready," Jamie-Lynn's mom told her after knocking lightly on her bedroom door before opening it.

Jamie-Lynn was lying on her bed, staring up at her ceiling, thinking about Annabelle. From the bedroom next to hers, she could hear her brother coughing something awful. It sounded like he would cough himself to death. She hated it when he got this bad. It was something she could never get used to.

Her brother's cystic fibrosis was yet another thing that made no sense. It was a curse her brother got from God when he was born. What could Ryan possibly have done to deserve it? He hadn't even been alive yet.

But Ryan's coughing wasn't enough to keep her from getting caught up in everything else. For a while, Jamie-Lynn was lost in memories. She didn't want to believe Annabelle was gone. She almost couldn't believe it. She still kept expecting the phone to ring and to hear Annabelle's voice on the other end, telling her it was all a big mix-up. There would be some funny story about what happened, and they would both laugh about it. Then Annabelle would come over and they'd bake cupcakes or something.

But the phone didn't ring.

Jamie-Lynn found herself becoming lost in what ifs. *What if Annabelle had been sick on Monday and not gone to school? What if she'd spent that Sunday night at Jamie-Lynn's and walked with her to school?* She'd done that before. Not very often, but it had happened. *What if a different person had been driving the school bus? What if the bus had been a minute later or a minute earlier? What if the driver of the eighteen-wheeler had waited for one more cup of coffee after breakfast? What if Annabelle had missed her school bus entirely because she was too slow getting ready?* Annabelle missed her bus at least once a month. *Why hadn't she missed* that *bus?*

"Did you hear me?" Jamie-Lynn's mom asked when Jamie-Lynn showed no sign of responding.

"I'm not hungry," Jamie-Lynn said without taking her eyes from her ceiling. Another cacophony of coughs erupted from Ryan's room. Her mom looked worriedly toward the sound, as though she could see her sick little boy lying helplessly in his bed right through the wall of Jamie-Lynn's room.

Jamie-Lynn had no idea how long ago she'd gotten home from school. Time didn't seem to work anymore.

Maybe it had been an hour, maybe more. Her mom was calling her for dinner, so probably it had been more.

It was Tuesday—the day after The Most Horrible of Days—and today wasn't any better than yesterday. If anything, it was even worse, because so many students, and even some teachers, acted so *normal*. Like everything was the same as before. She even saw people *smiling*. Kids *played* at lunch and recess. People were *happy*.

It was a normal day.

Except it *wasn't* normal. It wasn't normal because the desk beside Jamie-Lynn's had sat empty all day. It wasn't normal because at recess and lunch she sat by herself on a swing and just thought about everything while the swing beside her hung lifeless. Empty, just like that desk. It blew slightly in the light breeze, but try as she might, Jamie-Lynn couldn't make herself believe Annabelle was sitting in it.

It wasn't normal because life would never be normal again. It would always be limp and empty just like the swing and the desk.

It wasn't normal because you can't set your life back to 8:15 A.M. Monday morning and expect everything to just dry out and get back on the road and somehow work out okay.

Her mom knelt down beside her bed and touched her hair. "Honey, are you okay?"

Jamie-Lynn didn't answer.

"I'm worried about you."

"Why did she have to die?" Jamie-Lynn asked. Tears stood in her eyes. She asked the question more to the room than to her mom. It was a question that had been running through her mind underneath everything else ever since she found out about the accident yesterday morning.

"Oh honey," her mom said. "There is no answer to that. You'll make yourself crazy trying to find one."

"It makes no sense."

"Somewhere it does. You have to trust that it does."

Jamie-Lynn turned her head and stared at her mom's face, looking straight into her pale blue eyes. "How? How can it possibly make any sense?"

Her mom hesitated, as though she hadn't expected a response. Finally she said, "Annabelle's one of God's little angels now."

Jamie-Lynn turned back to her ceiling, slightly angry. "God should get His own angels," she said. "Or be happy with all the ones He has."

"I'm really worried about you."

Jamie-Lynn turned over on her side, facing away from her mother. Her hand clenched her bedspread.

"You sure you aren't hungry?"

Jamie-Lynn just nodded.

Her mom left her there on her bed, closing the bedroom door behind her.

The next day, Jamie-Lynn went to school but everything was just a blur of nothingness. There were no sounds, no smells, no tastes. All of the color of the world had drained away. She sat in class, looking out the window while the teacher droned on and on about various subjects. A robin flew onto the branch of a maple. It seemed to give Jamie-Lynn a sideways glance before continuing to the ground in search of something to eat. Jamie-Lynn gave it only the slightest attention.

The sky was a dull gray. The leaves on the trees had begun to fall, leaving the branches looking stark and naked. The grass was no longer a lush green. Under the sun, it would appear to be turning yellow, but under this sky it just looked like concrete.

The world was either dying or already dead, depending on where you looked.

To accentuate the point, the robin hopped over to the carcass of a dead rat and picked at its rotted fur. Was everyone's world like this, or just Jamie-Lynn's?

She heard her name. It sounded distant in her ears, but it pulled her from her thoughts. Her teacher, Miss Partridge, was saying it.

"Jamie-Lynn? Earth to Jamie-Lynn?"

Mechanically, Jamie-Lynn turned her head to the front of the class to where Miss Partridge stood with a pointer beside some math problem she'd written on the board. "Ah! So you are alive. Do you mind solving this for us?"

"I'm sorry," Jamie-Lynn said. "I can't."

"What do you mean?"

"Math problems aren't important anymore."

Ten minutes later, Jamie-Lynn found herself in the office of Mr. Dormer, the school counselor.

"I understand you were best friends with Annabelle Parks, one of the students who died in Monday's accident," Mr. Dormer said. He wore thin rimmed glasses, had very little hair, and looked skinny enough to have an eating disorder.

Jamie-Lynn barely listened. She looked down at the floor. She looked out his window. She looked at the shelves full of psychology books Mr. Dormer had lining most of the walls of his office, wondering if he'd really read them all, or if they were there just for show, or maybe intimidation. Finally she nodded.

"Her death must be very hard on you."

Jamie-Lynn didn't answer.

"Death is not an easy thing for anyone to deal with," Mr. Dormer said, "but it can be extra hard for girls of your age. Especially when it's such a surprising loss like this. You probably should see a grief counselor."

"I think I'm fine," Jamie-Lynn said. She spoke quietly and in monotone.

"Your teacher doesn't think you're fine."

"It's only been two days."

Mr. Dormer sat back in his chair, playing with a pencil between his fingers. "Can I ask what you think about when you think about Annabelle's death?"

A thousand things flashed through Jamie-Lynn's mind. What *didn't* she think about? She thought about *everything*. Her list of what-ifs, her projected life without her BFF by her side, how Annabelle died and somehow took the whole world with her, how there must be some way to bring her back again if Jamie-Lynn tried really hard, how she sometimes wished it was her that had been on the bus instead of Annabelle.

Not one of these were anything she would ever say out loud to anybody, though, especially not this freak.

So instead, she said, finally, "I think it's unfair."

"And life's supposed to be fair?" Mr. Dormer asked.

"Everything's fair," Jamie-Lynn said by force of habit. "All rules are on"

"What?"

"Nothing."

"Do you ever feel guilty?" Mr. Dormer asked.

"What do you mean?"

"Feel guilty about Annabelle's death?"

"No," Jamie-Lynn said. "Why should I feel guilty about it? I wasn't driving the bus." Truth was, though, she *did* feel guilty about it. *Often*. And it didn't make any sense.

"It's not uncommon for people to have survivor's guilt," Mr. Dormer said. "To feel guilty because they're alive and the person close to them isn't. It's not rational, but it's very common."

Jamie-Lynn said nothing.

Mr. Dormer talked a little longer, but nothing he said meant much to Jamie-Lynn. When he was finished, he called her mom and asked her to come pick Jamie-Lynn up. He told her he thought it was probably best for Jamie-Lynn to take some time off from school. At the very least she should stay home until the weekend, and maybe even take next week off, too.

"During this time," he stressed, "you should find her a proper grief counselor. I think she's having problems coping with Annabelle's death and really needs to see someone before things progress much further."

Jamie-Lynn's mother agreed.

Jamie-Lynn thought Mr. Dormer was a bit crazy. She also decided he hadn't read most of the books on those shelves.

4

Jamie-Lynn ended up taking more than just a couple of days off school. Her parents found her a real therapist — a psychologist named Angela Whitmore who specialized in child trauma. Jamie-Lynn saw her the day after she had been sent home by Mr. Dormer from his pretentious little office.

Angela, as the therapist asked Jamie-Lynn to call her, had a much nicer office than Mr. Dormer. She had books too, but not nearly as many as Mr. Dormer. She also had framed certificates stating she was a *real* psychologist and that she had probably at least glanced through most of the books at one time or another. Not that it mattered. Jamie-Lynn didn't care about the books, the office, the certificates, or Angela. She didn't want to be there. She wanted to be alone somewhere. Her dream was to fly high into the clouds where nobody was around her, and just scream as loud as she could. Then, when she was all screamed out, she would fall back to Earth and break every bone in her body. It sounded like a good way to die to Jamie-Lynn. Much better than drowning in a school bus.

"Your mom tells me you stay in your room a lot since the accident," Angela said. Jamie-Lynn's mom had sat with Angela alone for twenty minutes while Jamie-Lynn waited in the room outside the door. Then they changed places.

"I guess," Jamie-Lynn said.

Angela had black curly hair that hung down to her shoulders and wore glasses with thick red frames. She didn't appear much older than some of the university students Jamie-Lynn had seen. She wore a grey skirt and matching top and sat across from Jamie-Lynn. A small table made from white oak stood between them. It barely came up to Jamie-Lynn's knees.

There was a big cherry desk in the room with a plush chair on wheels, but for some reason Angela chose to talk to Jamie-Lynn here, where they both sat in the same type of chairs. Angela had her legs crossed with a yellow pad on her knee and a pen poised for taking notes. Jamie-Lynn didn't think there would be much need for note taking.

"I bet you lie there thinking about some pretty heavy stuff, hey?" Angela asked.

"Yeah." Jamie-Lynn spoke in the same monotone voice she had used with Mr. Dormer. She didn't spend much time looking at Angela. She looked more at the window over her shoulder through which the tops of three fir trees blew in a gentle breeze. Angela's office was on the third of a six floor office building.

"What do you think about?" Angela asked.

Jamie-Lynn wondered if every one of these counselor types were trained to ask the exact same questions. Mr. Dormer had gone straight to here, too.

"I dunno," she said.

"You *know* Annabelle's gone, though, right?"

This got her attention. "What do you mean?"

"You understand she's not coming back," Angela said. "That she died in that bus accident?"

Jamie-Lynn shifted uncomfortably in her seat. She subconsciously glanced over her shoulder to the closed door behind her where her mom waited. For some reason, this question made Jamie-Lynn uncomfortable. "Of course," she said. "She drowned."

Angela set her pen down on the paper. "Jamie," she said, "I know you know that *rationally*—"

"Jamie-*Lynn*," Jamie-Lynn corrected, cutting her off. She hated when people screwed up her name.

"Sorry. My mistake. "Jamie-Lynn, *rationally* you know your friend is gone, but *psychologically* it's not uncommon to be in denial about things. Even obvious things. I'm just trying to find out where you are in the grieving process."

"I know she drowned. I sat beside her empty desk all day at school," Jamie-Lynn felt herself tear up.

Angela sighed and pulled a tissue from a box on the table and passed it across. "I can't imagine how hard this is for you."

Balling the tissue up in her fist, both Jamie-Lynn's hands swung down. Her tear-filled eyes snapped to Angela's face. "Why did this have to happen? It makes no sense. It just makes me so . . . " She drifted off.

There was a silence while Angela waited for a word that would never come. Surprisingly, though, Angela successfully filled in the blank herself. "Angry?" she asked. "Upset? Mad? Hurt? All of the above?"

Jamie-Lynn stared at her, stunned. How did she know what she was going to say? It made no sense to feel the way Jamie-Lynn did. She shouldn't be angry that her best friend died, she should be sad. But all she felt was mad. And every hour she thought about the accident, it only got worse.

"Jamie-Lynn," Angela said, reaching across and touching her knee, "just so you know . . . what you're feeling is perfectly normal. There are five stages to the grieving process. Anger's probably the most pervasive of them all."

Jamie-Lynn sat there, listening. She said nothing.

"Everyone, no matter who you are, goes through all five steps when someone close to them dies. Sometimes you go through the steps in different order, often you go through them multiple times. Some people go through them fast. Some people take years. But everyone goes through them. You *have* to go through them. It's how we deal with death."

With a sigh, Jamie-Lynn allowed herself to feel something like relief for a moment. Until now, she had thought there was something wrong with her.

Angela pulled a sheet of paper out from under her pad and placed it on the table between them so that it faced Jamie-Lynn. It showed a circular graph with five pie slices displaying the different stages of grief. "This might help you. The steps are denial, anger, bargaining, depression, and, finally, acceptance. Generally, that's the order they're experienced in, but, like I said, not always. You're currently at anger."

"And that's normal?" Jamie-Lynn asked meekly. "After three days?"

Angela shrugged. "Time is different for everyone. It's normal for you."

Jamie-Lynn looked at the sheet. "What's bargaining?"

Angela nodded. "Yeah, depression and acceptance are pretty obvious. Bargaining is when you reach a point where you've accepted the death but aren't happy with the situation, so you decide to try and fix it."

"How can you fix something like this?"

"You might beg God to take your life in exchange for bringing Annabelle back, for instance."

If there was one thing Jamie-Lynn had come to a conclusion about over the past three days, it was that God wasn't about to make any nice deals that worked out in her favor. She had no faith He'd follow through with anything He promised to do.

Everywhere she looked she found evidence that God wasn't very nice.

5

Jamie-Lynn began losing track of time. Days folded into days. Psychologist appointments dissolved into psychologist appointments. She wasn't even sure how often she *went* to see Angela, but it seemed like that was all she did. She was either in her bedroom or in Angela Whitmore's office. If she was in her bedroom, she was either asleep, obsessed in her thoughts, or throwing some sort of angry fit.

She barely ate.

The time had a soundtrack: an underscore of staccato coughing fits that would come and go from Ryan's room. It was a really bad attack he was going through this time around, and it made everything worse. In the past, he'd had bad ones, but they rarely hung on this long. This one showed no sign of ending, and he'd already missed a lot of school. Jamie-Lynn wished he'd get well soon. Those days she didn't feel quite so full of rage or sorrow, she made her way into Ryan's room and spent time with him.

It was strange, but having a brother who had been sick all his life had somehow brought them closer. They never fought the way her friends fought with their siblings. She almost treated him like her own child. She grew up caring for him, reading to him, worrying about him. But worrying about Ryan at this time was just one more thing she didn't need in her head right now.

Jamie-Lynn's first big anger incident happened three days after her initial appointment with Angela Whitmore. She'd been in her usual spot, lying on top of her bed, staring at her ceiling, thinking about the injustice of everything. Only this time, she couldn't keep the rage from building up inside her. She thought about what Angela had said, about bargaining with God, and how much she now hated God for what he had done to Annabelle. God had taken her away and, in doing so, He'd also taken the world away. He had destroyed everything good in Jamie-Lynn's life.

It was so goddamn unfair. And it made her so mad she could no longer contain it. She picked up her prized baseball from her bedside table, the one she'd hit out of the park to win her little league series in what seemed like a lifetime of years ago (her dad had coached them that year), and, screaming, threw it as hard as she could. It hit the framed poster hanging on the wall across the room. The glass shattered into what seemed like a million pieces. The crash filled her room, drowning out Ryan's wet, wheezing coughs as the pieces showered to the floor.

Jamie-Lynn immediately felt better.

The noise brought her parents and even her sick brother running into her room to see what the hell was going on. When they found out, they didn't really know how to handle it, but Jamie-Lynn didn't care. Her mom and dad fumbled between being angry with her, and trying to be understanding and compassionate. Ryan seemed a little scared. Jamie-Lynn's mom returned him to his room and got him back into bed, while her dad swept up the glass in silence.

She just lay on her bed staring at the ceiling, *numb*.

When her parents had finally cleaned up all the glass, they gently closed Jamie-Lynn's bedroom door behind them as they quietly left. Jamie-Lynn thought they were just happy to finally escape.

Jamie-Lynn slept a lot. Right after that first incident with the baseball, her mom had taken her to their medical doctor and he gave her two prescriptions. Both were to help calm her down and relieve her anxiety. As a side effect, they also made her sleepy. This was great because she absolutely *loved* sleeping. Sleeping was the best. When Jamie-Lynn was asleep, all the problems of the world went away. Everything was right again. The dead spots rolled up like AstroTurf after the big game. But the second she woke up, it was like that split second before you hit the water, only in an alternate universe where you dive off the diving board and realize you've accidentally dove into a slab of concrete instead of a swimming pool.

The worst part, other than waking up, was *being* awake and lying there obsessing about things. Her thoughts spiraled out of control. She would think about Annabelle drowning, and, every time she did, she'd become so angry she'd just want to kill that bus driver.

Jamie-Lynn continued throwing things. Her parents seemed to get used to it. It wasn't long until they just ignored the behavior. Sometimes Ryan would come in and ask if everything was all right.

"Yeah," Jamie-Lynn would say.

"You sure?" he would ask again and then start coughing.

"Go back to bed."

And he would go. Throwing things made her feel better. Breaking things made her feel better. Besides, it was only *her* stuff she was throwing and breaking, and it was only "stuff". It wasn't worth anything. It was useless. It couldn't bring Annabelle back. She couldn't believe she ever cared about all this "stuff" she had anyway.

Pretty soon her life became a routine of sleeping, obsessing, raging, breaking, rinsing and repeating. She hated who she was. She hated her life. She felt trapped. She couldn't even remember what it felt like to actually be alive anymore. Somehow though, through all this, she felt closer to Annabelle. Maybe it was because she felt more dead than ever.

This was what she had become. She thought it would be like this for the rest of her life.

That was until that one day came when everything changed.

6

Jamie-Lynn woke up in a hospital bed.

She thought back. She couldn't remember coming into the hospital.

She thought back harder. The last thing she remembered was being in her room. She may have been sleeping; she couldn't really recall. Everything ran together. It was all just gray and coughing and wheezing and sadness and anger. With flashes of red.

She tried sitting up, but she couldn't. She tried to move her arms, but she couldn't. When she looked at them, she realized why: they were strapped down to the sides of the bed. There was a big white bandage around her left wrist and an IV running into her right one. The fluorescent lights overhead were bright and flickered, casting everything in that sterile bone white color that always made hospitals feel so icky when you visited them. The curtains on both sides of her bed were pulled closed. They were baby blue and the walls a light yellow. Both colors looked particularly pukey under this light.

An uneasy feeling filled her stomach. It was bad enough waking up somewhere and not knowing how you got there. It was even worse waking up tied to a hospital bed with no idea why. She didn't like being strapped down at all. It made her feel so helpless.

A table with wheels ran alongside her bed. On it was a vase with flowers. They looked new. Two roses, a daisy, a tulip, and two other ones she didn't know. The roses were yellow and pink and looked much better than the curtains and the wall. Two chairs sat empty on the other side of her bed. One had a half-folded newspaper on it. A paper coffee cup from Starbucks stood on the table beside the chair.

Someone had been sitting there recently.

She jumped as a person came around the curtain. "Ah, I see my young patient is finally awake." It was a doctor in a white jacket and brown pants with a stethoscope around his neck. He looked maybe twenty-five and was clean shaven with neat black hair and brown eyes. In his hand was a clipboard.

"Let's let some light in here, shall we?" He pulled the curtain on her right open, revealing a wall full of windows that looked outside. The sky was partially cloudy but bright, and the daylight added a welcoming addition to the horrible fluorescents.

"Why am I tied down?" Jamie-Lynn asked. She had a few questions ready to go, but that one made its way out first.

"Just to be safe," the doctor said. He looked at the top page on his clipboard and then flipped to the one below it. Then he looked up at her and smiled. "Jamie-Lynn Howard, correct?"

Jamie-Lynn nodded.

"I'm doctor Baker." He had a slight British accent.

"Can you untie me?"

He scratched his head above his eye. "Not just yet. We need to get that approval."

"Approval? What are you talking about? Approval from who?"

"Your psychiatrist. A Doctor . . . " He flipped through his pages again. "A Dr. Porter. Good guy, actually."

"What happened? Why am I here?"

He crossed his arms. One hand came to his chin, it still held his pen. "You don't remember?"

"I have no idea," she said. "I woke up and here I am, tied to a bed in a hospital."

"You were brought in last night."

"Why?"

He glanced out the window as though considering how to answer. Or maybe he was thinking about whether or not he *would* answer. "Really you should be talking to Dr. Porter about this," he said.

"He's not here," she said. "And I'm going to start freaking out if you don't tell me."

"All right. Jamie-Lynn, you tried to kill yourself last night."

She looked at the bandage around her wrist. "No way. I'd remember something like that."

Doctor Baker went back to his notes. "I wasn't attending when you came in, but apparently you had cuts on your wrist that had been made with broken glass. They were pretty deep. You received sixteen stitches."

Oh. My. God, Jamie-Lynn thought. How could she not remember any of this? And how could she have tried to kill herself? It didn't seem possible, at least right now. "Why can't you untie my arms?"

"There's a few reasons. Mainly we have to wait for Dr. Porter to do a risk evaluation."

"Risk of what?"

He paused before answering. "Of how much of a threat you are to yourself and whether or not you're going to try and run out of here if we give you the chance."

Jamie-Lynn's restraints were removed two hours later.

She wound up spending three days in the hospital and came out with two souvenirs: a scar on her inside left wrist she would have the rest of her life, and a third prescription to add to her ever-growing collection. This one was for some kind of antidepressant.

Jamie-Lynn didn't really care about either one. She didn't really care about anything. Nothing mattered.

The antidepressants turned out to be a pleasant surprise. They actually worked fairly well, although she thought they weren't very well named. They didn't really make you any less depressed so much as they just made you more numb than ever to the world around you. Just when she had thought she couldn't care any less about things, the doctor went and gave her a pill that proved her wrong.

Now she *truly* didn't care. And it was a vast improvement over having even the slightest hatred toward anything.

So the world was now completely and terminally dead, and it felt just as dead as it looked. At least things

were starting to make a little sense. They had some con-
sistency to them.

This change in her was considered an improvement
by everyone around her. Enough that she even started
going back to school.

7

She didn't know how long it had been since the new boy
started attending Rainforest Elementary. He had started
while she was away and she'd missed so many days that
she'd lost count. She had no idea how many had gone
by—at times it felt like a week, at other times it felt like a
month. It was like time had been submerged in water
and was being influenced by the ebb and flow of the
currents, moving slowly back and forth like seaweed.

The new boy's name was Joel Kenyan, and she esti-
mated he must have appeared in her class sometime in
the two weeks following the Most Horrible Of All Days,
while she was at home throwing stuff around her room.

Joel Kenyan was one of those people you knew
instantly that everyone else probably liked very much.
He was good-natured, easy to get along with, happy,
warm, caring, and an all-around good guy. In the little
bit of time he'd been attending Rainforest Elementary,
Jamie-Lynn could tell he'd already built a circle of
friends bigger than she had, and she'd been at the same
school for eight years.

Everyone liked Joel Kenyan.

Except Jamie-Lynn. She hated him.

She didn't like the way the light twinkled in his icy
blue eyes, or the way his skin shone under the sun, but

mainly she couldn't stand the way he smiled. His smile radiated warmth and happiness. His smile was alive in a way that made her want to punch out every one of his bright white teeth.

She hated that he *could* smile like that.

How dare he?

In a world full of death and dead things, he stood out like a bright spot of color on a black canvas. What's more, Jamie-Lynn didn't like the way everything felt slightly unbalanced when Joel Kenyan was around. And he *always* seemed to be around. He was a weird kid, and her life was weird enough, thank you very much. If anyone wanted proof, she had the scar on her wrist to prove it.

Jamie-Lynn tried as best she could to stay as far away from Joel Kenyan as possible.

At lunch that day, a situation occurred in the hallway outside her classroom. Derek Schulz, probably the closest thing to a school bully Rainforest Elementary had, was trying to put Cody Taylor's head into one of the toilets in the washroom and flush it. Cody was probably the same height as Derek, but Derek had at least twenty pounds on him.

Cody was putting up a good fight, though. When Jamie-Lynn got there, Cody wasn't even in the washroom yet. Every time Derek grabbed him and dragged him toward the door, Cody would struggle and pull his way free, trying to get away. But Derek would inevitably grab him again before he got very far, and slide him just a wee bit closer to that door.

Every second, more and more kids gathered around. There must have been at least twenty by the time Jamie-Lynn got there. Jamie-Lynn wondered if everyone was going to follow them into the washroom once the two boys got inside and just crowd around and watch Cody get his head flushed. He'd already had his fingers slammed into the door once, and it looked like his face was bleeding.

"Will you leave him alone?" Jamie-Lynn called out to Derek. The antidepressants were still leaving her dead to most things, but she still hated injustice. Unfairness always got to her.

"Shut up!" Derek yelled back at her.

"You're such a loser," Jamie-Lynn said.

Just then, that creepy Joel Kenyan joined the crowd. He radiated weirdness all the way from where he was on the other side of the circle. Jamie-Lynn could literally *feel* him standing there. He was so odd. She looked around, wondering if anyone else felt this way about him. If they did, nobody showed it. Nobody else was paying much attention to Joel Kenyan. They were all too wrapped up in waiting for Cody to get flushed.

Jamie-Lynn couldn't watch any more of this play out. She felt herself getting angry and decided to let Derek have it one more time before leaving. "Just let him the hell go! There's enough horribleness in the world! All you're doing is adding to it, you jerk!"

She expected Derek to come back with a whopper insult this time. He wouldn't be able to stand being chastised like that in front of all these students. By a girl, no less.

But it didn't work out the way she expected.

Derek sort of stopped pulling on Cody and slowly turned and looked at her. Then a strange thing happened. His grip on the back of Cody's shirt loosened, and he actually let him go. Even Cody seemed surprised, he looked at Derek for an explanation.

"She's right," Derek said quietly to Cody. "Go. Before I change my mind."

Wow. Now *that* was unexpected. Jamie-Lynn felt something through the haze of anti-depressants and anti-anxiety meds that she hadn't in a long time. She wasn't even sure what it was. Maybe "hope" was the word she was looking for.

The rest of the day was spent lost in thought. At first those thoughts involved mulling over what had happened outside the bathroom, but soon her thoughts turned in the direction they always did; one that ultimately lead to Annabelle. By the end of the day, Jamie-Lynn had forgotten all about her small respite of hope, and was once again overwhelmed by tragedy. Thankfully, the antidepressants kept most of her feelings a fair distance away.

Walking home, Jamie-Lynn felt as bad as ever. The only good part was that things couldn't get much worse.

And just like every time she tried to find a silver lining, she turned out to be dead wrong. Because in the next moment, Jamie-Lynn learned that eerie Joel Kenyan lived just one street over from her.

This meant he walked virtually the same route she did to and from school at virtually the same time she did every day. When she discovered this, she shuddered. She could barely stand being within a hundred yards of the kid without having a bizarre feeling of uneasiness wash over her. She hated looking at him. Now, every day she had to risk seeing him on the sidewalk. Twice.

Why wouldn't fate stop throwing crap curveballs at her? Life was hard enough. God kept making it worse.

She decided to take matters into her own hands and make sure their paths never crossed; Jamie-Lynn started coming to school twenty minutes earlier than usual and staying twenty minutes later. It was a bit of a pain, but she used the time to catch up on her homework, so it wasn't all in vain. Besides, if she wasn't at school, she'd just be lying around wallowing in her own sorrow anyway.

This plan worked perfectly for two mornings and two afternoons in a row. On the third morning, though, she ran into trouble.

Trouble came in the form of a stray dog. Normally dogs and Jamie-Lynn got along fine. And normally—in her neighborhood—any dogs not on a leash, or behind a fence, were nice dogs. And usually dogs were out for walks with their owners. You didn't often see them wandering the streets by themselves.

This dog wasn't on a leash, or behind a fence, or with any sort of escort. To make matters worse, it showed every sign of not being a very nice dog.

Jamie-Lynn didn't have much of a chance to avoid it. It came at her from behind a large thorny bush at the very edge of the sidewalk, so she hadn't seen it from any distance. As soon as she walked past the bush it started barking and snarling. Jamie-Lynn saw its sharp teeth. Foam appeared at its mouth. It scared her nearly to death; her heart leapt up into her ribcage and pounded against her ribs at double speed.

The dog was only a few feet away from her, gnashing wildly. She didn't know what kind of dog it was, but it was big. Jamie-Lynn thought, if it were to stand up on its hind legs, it would probably be just as tall as she was.

She was so scared, she couldn't move (other than shake). Standing there frozen with fear, she had no idea what to do. She couldn't remember ever feeling this afraid. If she ran, she thought for sure it would leap on her. After all, everyone knew that dogs could smell fear. But if she stayed where she was, it looked like it was going to attack her any minute. She kept waiting for it to lunge at any moment.

Frantically, she looked around for anyone, but there was nobody. There weren't even any other students on the street. Nobody else went to school twenty minutes early. Nobody else hated Joel Kenyan that much.

Then, maybe a block or two down away, she saw someone coming down the sidewalk. Her heart thundered in her chest. She couldn't make out who it was, but the prospect of anyone coming to save her was almost too good to be true. She just hoped they would get here in time.

Jamie-Lynn's attention kept going back and forth between the dog's frothing mouth snarling and snapping and the person walking toward her. As he drew closer, she could see it was a boy. And he was whistling.

This confused her. Surely he could hear the dog? The dog was so loud she was surprised that the neighbors hadn't come outside yet to see what was going on.

The boy drew even closer.

She felt him before she recognized him.

It was Joel Kenyan. With his perfect hair, and crystal blue eyes. Why had he left home early today? Was he *trying* to run into her? Those were crazy thoughts. Besides, today she was actually happy to see him. Hopefully he wouldn't just run away when he saw the dog. It didn't look like he was about to—he was definitely close enough now to hear the growling and barking, yet he showed no sign of turning tail. He was still whistling. Or at least appeared to be. Jamie-Lynn couldn't *hear* any whistling anymore. Not over the barking.

Then a terrible thought occurred to her: what were two seventh graders going to do about this dog anyway? Odds were they'd just both get attacked. She still kept waiting for Joel Kenyan to somehow notice the obvious dog and turn around and run away.

But he didn't. He kept coming closer. And closer.

And closer.

Until he was standing right beside Jamie-Lynn. He looked at the dog gnashing its teeth. It looked ready to attack. Jamie-Lynn's pulse sped up faster. Sweat trickled down the back of her neck. She felt the hairs on her arm stand straight up.

"You okay?" Joel asked her.

As he spoke, the dog made its last bark. Then it stopped snapping its jaws.

"T . . . this dog . . . it's going to b . . . bite me," Jamie-Lynn stammered. She was shaky. Her knees wobbled. Her legs felt like Jello.

"No, it's all bark, I think," Joel said. He reached out and patted the top of the dog's head. Jamie-Lynn thought he was nuts. She almost pulled his arm back, but didn't want to put any of her body parts any closer to those teeth.

But the dog just sat back on its haunches and whimpered.

Jamie-Lynn couldn't believe it. "H . . . how did you do that?"

Joel shrugged. "Animals get along with me. Going to school early?"

She nodded.

"Me too. Wanna walk together?"

She realized after what he'd just done for her she really had no choice. Still shaken up, she answered, "Sh . . . Sure. I guess."

8

As the autumn days rolled by, the numbness that filled Jamie-Lynn didn't change much. Surprisingly, it was improved somewhat by her walks to and from school with Joel Kenyan which continued after the "dog incident". She still felt a strangeness when she was close to him, almost as though he emitted some sort of tangible emotion, but she no longer classified it as something "weird in a *bad* way". It had been promoted to simply "weird".

They didn't have much in common, but at least he gave her someone to walk with. Walking alone had just been a constant reminder that Annabelle was gone, even though Jamie-Lynn rarely walked to school with Annabelle. Anytime she was alone, Annabelle was still all Jamie-Lynn thought about.

Over the past little while, Jamie-Lynn's anger had subsided substantially. She hadn't had a fit full of rage for quite some time. She wasn't sure if that meant she had gotten through that part of the grieving process, or if all of the drugs she was taking were just blocking her ability to feel angry. They seemed to be blocking most other feelings.

When they first started walking together, her and Joel didn't really talk much. They either walked along in silence or, quite often, to the tune of Joel Kenyan quietly whistling. This wasn't nearly as annoying as Jamie-Lynn would've thought if someone had told her he was a whistler before their walks started. He actually whistled better than anyone she'd ever heard before. His notes all sounded in tune and had a bird-like quality to them. He also seemed to have a keen sense of knowing when Jamie-Lynn really wanted silence, and on those days, he didn't whistle.

All in all, Joel Kenyan turned out to be a pretty good walking companion.

This made Jamie-Lynn happy. Well, as happy as she could be right now. She had worried he might turn out to be one of those kids you couldn't shut up who always wanted to talk about whatever happened to be on their mind, or make you listen to every single detail of what they did last night, but he wasn't like that at all. If she didn't talk, he rarely did either. If she did say something, he would politely carry on his side of the conversation, but never take it over, or push things in a direction that made Jamie-Lynn uncomfortable.

That was until one day.

On that day he suddenly seemed to change his whole modus operandi. It happened about a week and a half after he saved her from the dog.

"Do you mind if I ask you something?" he said, breaking the silence. It had been one of those mornings when Jamie-Lynn wanted to think about life, and Joel had been gracious enough to know without being told that he shouldn't whistle, or even make the slightest odd noise along the way. But now, here he was actually inducing conversation.

She sighed. "What?"

"Well I heard about the bus accident that happened before I moved here . . . "

Jamie-Lynn almost gasped. Not only was he forcing her to talk, he was doing it on the last subject in the world she wanted to discuss with him. She didn't know how to tell him this. Her brain was immediately a tangle of jumbled electrical wires.

" . . . and I just wondered if you ever think about all those kids? I wasn't even here, and I think about it all the time, you know?" They went on a few steps before he continued. "It was horrible. I've only heard the odd detail, but I can't believe what happened. Do you ever . . . do you ever wonder what happens to kids when they die all of a sudden like that? All together?"

She absolutely could not believe he just asked her that question. How could she possibly answer him? She didn't want to show a reaction. She started to sweat. A pressure built up behind her eyes and, for a second, she thought she might even cry even though she was taking meds that absolutely forbade crying of any sort. "I . . . I don't know."

"Were any of them your friends?"

She stopped walking and just stared at the ground in front of her. Her fingers were still wrapped around the backpack straps that hung over her shoulders. "Yes. Joel," she answered very flatly. "Why are you asking me all this?"

"Because I'm interested. Am I upsetting you?"

Yes. Yes. Yes. "No," she lied. "I lost my best friend. Her name was Annabelle."

"I'm sorry," he said. "Do you still think about it a lot?"

She turned and stared at him and actually felt a tear roll down her cheek. "Do I *think* about it? I never *stop* thinking about it. Look at this." She held out her wrist but he didn't look, he just kept starting at her face. "Look!" she almost screamed it.

"I don't have to," he said quietly.

"I never, *ever* stop thinking about it, and I don't think I ever will! She was my best friend and it was just so . . . so . . . *unfair*. It makes no sense. Nothing makes any sense. Life makes no sense!" She started to shake. "You know what my mom told me after? After it happened? She said Annabelle was 'one of God's little angels now'! How pathetic is that? I just can't . . . " She lowered her head and her voice went quiet with it. "I need this to make sense."

They stood there in silence for what felt like an eternity to Jamie-Lynn until finally Joel said, "Life appears not to make any sense a lot, but I think in reality, if we could see everything—how it all works, all at once—I think it would make perfect sense. I'm really sorry about your friend, and I'm really sorry about how you feel."

"You have no idea how I feel," she said.

Calmly Joel said, "You don't know that. You don't know what I know."

She thought about this. Sniffling, she wiped her nose and apologized. "You're right, I'm sorry."

"I also know you'll get through this one day and things will be okay again. They'll never be the *same* as they were, but life is never the same as it was. Everything changes. Life's all about change."

She blinked. Who was this kid? Suddenly it was like talking to the Buddha. Jamie-Lynn could barely keep up with what he was telling her. He sounded so . . . so . . . old. And knowledgeable. He somehow made her feel better. In two minutes, Joel Kenyan managed to make her feel a hundred times better about everything than Angela Whitmore had been able to do through dozens of sessions.

She felt that aura radiate from him again. Only this time it wasn't just "weird" but almost "good weird" and she knew it underscored what he had said. It had been important. He had interrupted her wish for a silent walk because he knew she needed to hear what he had to say and she had needed to hear it now.

He certainly came off much older than a seventh grader. Although, with his fair features and almost porcelain face, he could pass for someone younger. Joel Kenyan was definitely a paradox.

"Thank you," she said, wiping her eyes with her sleeve.

They continued on to school. For the rest of the walk, Jamie-Lynn got the silence she wanted, so she remained lost in thought. Only, instead of thinking of Annabelle, she thought of everything Joel had just told her.

As autumn drew to a close, Jamie-Lynn's walks to school with Joel became less quiet. They talked more and more and almost always wound up talking about how Jamie-Lynn felt about Annabelle. Her trust in Joel Kenyan grew to the point where she almost felt like she had Annabelle back in some ways.

Something else was happening as she got closer to Joel Kenyan. And this was something that could never have happened with Annabelle.

Jamie-Lynn's heart was opening up to him. Joel was slowly bringing life back to her world, and the epicenter of that life glowed from inside of him. It made him very important to her. The degree of importance was something Jamie-Lynn herself didn't really understand at first.

It was like having a seed planted in your yard and not knowing it was there. At first, you're barely even aware of the stalk poking through the soil. But after a little rain, and some sunlight, buds begin appearing.

And then they open their colorful petals to the world, and you can no longer ignore the beauty that's been there all along.

In the same way, there came a point when Jamie-Lynn could no longer deny the feelings she had for Joel Kenyan. She started to realize they existed when he began appearing in her dreams. Dreams are always dead giveaways because you can't control them. They're your mind's way of telling you things when you need to be hit on the head with a baseball bat before you get it.

It was funny. When she first met Joel Kenyan, everyone seemed to be his friend. Except her.

Now once again, she didn't feel like his friend. That had stopped sometime in the last couple of weeks. Somehow her feelings for him had transformed into something else.

Something bigger and brighter.

Jamie-Lynn Howard was falling for Joel Kenyan.

9

"Wanna come over to my place for a while?" Jamie-Lynn asked Joel on their way home a few days later. It was a Monday afternoon and the sky was completely clear, but saturated with the smell of dampness the way it could get this time of year. There was a small breeze at their backs, and it almost felt as though life itself wanted to help Jamie-Lynn along the way.

"Okay," Joel said. "Will anyone be home?"

"Probably my mom. My dad will still be at work. And my little brother. But he'll be in his room. He's sick, so he stays in bed." She stopped to tie the shoe-lace of one of her pink Converse sneakers.

"How long's he been sick?"

She frowned. "Ten years."

"Yikes. I'm assuming that's most of his life, then?"

"Yeah. He's got cystic fibrosis. He's not always this bad, though. Usually he goes to school and stuff, but this attack's been terrible. He's been home for probably a month now. I'm kind of worried about him." She stood and they continued walking.

Joel didn't say anything, he just seemed to go inside his own head for a while, as though he was completely lost in some other world. This was a turn of the tables on Jamie-Lynn and how it was when they first started their school walks. She decided not to talk, and give him the same quiet time he had given her back then.

Jamie-Lynn lived in a three level house on Silverwood Drive. It had a quaint front yard with a couple of Japanese maple trees and a trimmed hedge that ran along the edges. Wooden steps led up to the front door, but only company ever went into the house that way. Jamie-Lynn had to go in through the back, which meant following a gravel path around the garage.

When they got inside, they found her mom doing laundry, tossing clothes into the washing machine. You had to walk through the laundry room to get from the back door to anywhere else, so there was no avoiding introducing Mom to Joel. Not that Jamie-Lynn intended on avoiding her.

"Hi Mom," she said, kicking off her sneakers. "This is my friend, Joel."

Her mom seemed surprised, only Jamie-Lynn wasn't sure if the surprise came from the fact that Joel was a boy, or because she called him her friend. This was the first time since Annabelle's death that Jamie-Lynn showed any interest in another human being.

"It's very nice to meet you, Joel," Jamie-Lynn's mom said. She was about three inches taller than Jamie-Lynn, and had very blonde hair that was up in a bun today. She had on pajama pants and an extra-large T-shirt that probably once belonged to Jamie-Lynn's dad.

The kids shuffled past into the kitchen. "Go ahead and fix yourself a sandwich or something if you want," Jamie-Lynn's mom called out behind them.

"You hungry?" Jamie-Lynn asked Joel.

"Not really," he said.

"Wanna watch TV?"

"I don't care. Whatever."

From upstairs, Ryan began coughing terribly. It came out of nowhere, but it was one of those thick, wet chain of coughs that sounded like it would never let up. It got deeper and louder, finding its way down the stairs and through the floor, filling up the house. It was a sound you *never* got used to. Jamie-Lynn hated it. She would give practically anything to take that cough away from her brother. Many times she had lay there in her bed, listening to him in the next room sounding like he was only moments away from death, wishing with all her heart that God would let her trade him places.

But He wouldn't. Life's not like that. Life's not fair.

Everything's fair. All rules are on. Oh, if only her and Annabelle had seen the reality of how wrong they were with their stupid little phrase.

She thought about Annabelle then, but for the first time since her death it wasn't in a bad way. She wondered what Annabelle would think about Jamie-Lynn bringing a boy home? She'd probably flip. She'd definitely want details the second he left, that's for sure. Jamie-Lynn wondered if she'd like Joel. She wondered if she'd have felt the creepy weirdness thing from him the same way Jamie-Lynn did. Nobody else seemed to. Yet Jamie-Lynn still felt emotions radiate from Joel, only they weren't creepy and weird anymore, they were all happy and nice and yummy.

The coughing grew worse before it finally stopped. Jamie-Lynn looked at Joel almost apologetically, expecting to see a different expression on his face than the one he wore. She wasn't sure what she *had* expected, but surely listening to someone sounding like that had to be an unpleasant experience. So she expected him to react in a way someone hearing an unpleasant thing would react.

But Joel's face showed no signs of anything like that. What it showed was a deep understanding, full of love and compassion. And it wasn't just in his face. Like everything else about Joel Kenyan, it radiated from him like beams blasting off the surface of the sun.

In that moment she could have kissed him.

"Can I meet your brother?" he asked.

His question caught her by surprise. She even stumbled on her answer. "Um, yeah," she stammered. "Of course. He'd love to meet you. Come on."

She led him upstairs to Ryan's room. By the time they reached the top, Ryan was coughing again, although he wasn't nearly as bad as before. But there was still that wet quality to the coughs, like his lungs were full of water that just wouldn't leave. It made him sound sixty years old, not ten.

Quietly, Jamie-Lynn knocked on her brother's door and asked if it was okay if she came in and introduced him to her new friend.

Between coughs, Ryan sat up a little and said, "Yeah." Like her mom, he seemed surprised to see a new face. Or, more likely in Ryan's case, he was probably surprised that he was being introduced to one of Jamie-Lynn's friends in such a formal manner.

"Ryan, this is Joel Kenyan. Joel, Ryan."

Ryan coughed a few times. Unlike Jamie-Lynn, Ryan looked more like Mom than Dad. He had a shock of blonde hair that was never combed (especially when he was stuck in bed) and big red lips. Jamie-Lynn's lips were thin, like her dad's. Ryan's eyes were blue, but they didn't shine ice water the way Joel's did. Right now, they were wet with the tears brought on from the pressure of all the coughing. Jamie-Lynn could tell her brother was purposely holding back his coughs as he sat up even taller and the two boys shook hands.

"My pleasure," said Joel.

But Ryan could only go without coughing so long and then the water in his lungs overwhelmed him. An explosion of coughs let go, racking his body. He shook and rocked back and forth, snatching wheezing breaths between coughs when he could. Jamie-Lynn looked worriedly from Ryan to Joel. But Joel kept his eyes fixed on Ryan and not with an expression of worry, but with that same look of love, compassion, and understanding he had downstairs.

Jamie-Lynn could barely stand to be in the room when Ryan was this bad.

"I'm . . . really . . . sorry . . . " Ryan managed to get out through the coughs. They were controlling him. Jamie-Lynn couldn't believe he could manage to even talk at all. "This . . . is . . . really . . . embarrassing."

Joel squatted beside the bed. "Oh no, no. It's not embarrassing. This is nothing to be embarrassed about. Here, it might be easier if you lie yourself back down."

Gently, he reached out his left hand and, putting his palm on Ryan's chest, pushed him down so he was lying on the bed. Jamie-Lynn almost told him not to touch her brother while he's like that because usually it's better for the coughing if he's vertical, but something told her to let Joel do it.

She was glad she did, because literally ten seconds later, Ryan's coughing and wheezing began to slow.

"There. Easy now," Joel said, quietly and calmly. His hand still on Ryan's chest.

There were a few more coughs. Each one quieter than the last. Each one dryer. Ryan's lungs were emptying of fluid. It wasn't long before he stopped coughing entirely.

His lungs hadn't sounded this dry in a month. Ryan had gone without coughing for some periods of time, but it had never just stopped like this.

It was a miracle.

Jamie-Lynn looked at Joel wide-eyed. "How did you do that?"

"I didn't do anything."

"Yes you did. You touched him and made him stop coughing."

"No. I touched him and he happened to stop coughing."

"That's not what *I* saw." She stared at him. "You . . . what . . . ?"

"What?" Joel asked.

But she couldn't form the question she wanted to ask. She didn't really know what it was.

They spent most of the rest of Joel's visit in Jamie-Lynn's bedroom talking. Joel stayed for another hour and a half, during which Ryan slept more soundly than Jamie-Lynn could remember him sleeping in a long time. Not once did he wake up coughing.

After Joel finally left, Jamie-Lynn went downstairs to the kitchen where her mom had started cooking spaghetti for dinner. "Your friend seems nice," Mom said.

"Yeah," Jamie-Lynn said. But more importantly: "Ryan stopped coughing."

Her mom smiled. "I *know* isn't it *great*? Maybe he's getting better again. I sure hope so."

Ryan didn't wake up coughing all through that night. The next day, he coughed a little, but they were normal coughs. Not deathly wet, house shaking coughs.

Three days later he was back at school, as good as ever.

And Jamie-Lynn still didn't believe what Joel had told her. There was no way Ryan's coughing coming to an end and Joel touching him the way he had at the exact same time was a coincidence. She had *been* there. She saw the way Joel looked at her brother.

She saw it with her own eyes.

It was a miracle.

One thing was certain: there was something more than odd about Joel Kenyan.

10

The morning Jamie-Lynn woke from the Big Dream was the morning she had to completely give in to the fact that it had happened. In her dream, he had kissed her and, in a world that was full of death barely a month ago, there were suddenly rainbows, and butterflies, and unicorns. Jamie-Lynn woke up feeling like a little girl again. And the feeling didn't run away like a wild horse heading for a distant hill the way the dreams all had right after Annabelle died. This time it stayed. She woke up feeling alive, and she stayed alive.

And there was only one reason why she was alive.

She loved him.

Everybody seemed to like him, but she *loved* him. Nobody could possibly love him as much as she, for, when she thought about it now, nothing else had really filled her head during the last handful of days and those portions of the night she lay in bed unable to sleep, staring up at her ceiling, thinking about his crystal blue eyes and his tender features.

And she knew something about Joel Kenyan that nobody else knew. While nobody around here, anyway. That's for certain.

She had suspected for a little while now, but it had seemed so far-fetched, she couldn't bring herself to actually believe it. Thinking through everything now, there could be no other possibility. It was the only thing that made perfect sense.

Joel Kenyan had a secret.

An awesome secret.

Another thing she noticed was that lately, while she was busy falling in love with Joel, her mourning for Annabelle had quietly ceased. She had moved on to silent acceptance as Angela would probably put it. Jamie-Lynn hadn't even noticed it happening, and now it was too late because it was over. And thinking about it like that made her feel strange—as though she had somehow betrayed her best friend by forgetting to mourn her death any longer than she had. But she could mourn no more. She was done with the grieving process, and once one is done, one is done. It wasn't something that could be consciously controlled, at least not by Jamie-Lynn.

The walk to school that morning was a weird one. Jamie-Lynn felt lighter than air. Joel seemed to glow under the autumn dawn. She couldn't stop smiling. They spoke very little, and he kept looking at her strangely. She wanted to take his hand, to wrap him in her arms, to kiss him, but she didn't have that kind of courage. So she just thought about these things while he walked beside her, a couple of feet away.

Then, in the afternoon, Joel met her after school as he always did, by her locker. Only this time he asked her something peculiar. "Is it all right if we stay behind today?"

"Stay behind where?"

"Here," he said. "By the lockers. Until after everyone is gone. I'd like to talk with you about something."

She swallowed. A sickness came to her stomach. "I guess." She understood. Joel Kenyan's awesome secret might not be so awesome after all.

Around her, kids put on their coats and piled on their backpacks. Locker doors slammed closed, locks twisted around, and small groups sped off for the outside world in a flurry of excitement. Jamie-Lynn noticed kids were a lot faster when it came to getting out of the school than they were in the morning when it came to coming in.

When the last one had left, and the hall door swung closed behind him, Jamie-Lynn let her back slide down the front of her locker until she was sitting cross-legged on the floor. Joel sat down beside her. She didn't look at him. Her eyes remained focused on her pink sneakers which were grass-stained and had different colored laces, one purple and one yellow.

"I know what you are," she said.

He said nothing.

"You don't have to tell me. It's obvious now. I realized it last night before bed, but couldn't bring myself to believe it until today. But I know. I think I've known for a while."

Still he said nothing.

"And now that we're here, it worries me," she said.

There was more silence and then he finally spoke. "Why?"

"Because," she said. "I'm afraid."

"Of . . . ?"

She turned and looked at him for the first time since they sat down. She hated the way the fluorescent lights shone off his cheeks making his face look so soft and fragile. So . . . angelic. "That you're going to leave."

"Nothing lasts forever," he said.

She sighed. "Especially not people," she said, her eyes searching his. "Will it happen soon?"

He nodded ever so slightly. "You don't need me anymore. You understand."

"I need you more than ever," she pleaded.

"No," he said softly. "You don't. You're safe now. You've learned to love again. You'd forgotten."

She scrunched up her face. "How do you forget something like that?" she asked.

"Easy," he said. "You just do. But your heart doesn't. It always remembers." He reached out and touched her ear and smiled. "You just had to relearn how to listen to your heart again. That's all."

She didn't return his smile. Instead, she nearly pouted as her arms crossed defiantly. "Why do I lose everyone I love? It's not fair!"

His voice went even softer. "You're thinking of it all wrong and completely upside down. What you should

be asking yourself is why are you so lucky to keep getting opportunities to love? Think of how many people
there are that don't. Especially at your age."

"I don't feel lucky."

"I know," he said. "But you don't feel angry anymore, either."

She uncrossed her arms. He was right, she didn't
feel angry anymore. She felt okay. Even though he was
leaving, she was going to be okay. Her eyes moved from
the floor to his face. There was a wetness to his eyes that
seemed to go on forever and, knowing what she knew,
maybe it did. She wondered how old he really was.
Eons?

"No," she said. "I'm not angry. Is this it then?"

He nodded.

"So where are you . . . ? Oh, I guess you can't tell me
that, right?"

"You wouldn't be able to understand if I tried," he
said, and somehow that made perfect sense.

She looked down at his lips. Like the rest of his face,
they looked soft. She felt herself automatically moving
closer.

Then, in the next moment, they kissed and it felt as
though the world had exploded beneath her. If she had
any doubts about whether or not she'd learned to love
again, this kiss was putting them all to bed.

When he broke the embrace, he said quietly, "It's
time," and stood up.

She remained seated on the floor. "So are you
headed . . . ?" And she rolled her eyes skyward.

He laughed. "You watch too many movies. Goodbye Jamie-Lynn, it was my absolute pleasure learning about your life."

"Goodbye Joel Kenyan," she said. "If that's your real name." She giggled. "Maybe I'll see you again one day?"

He shrugged. "Only one person knows that for sure."

Jamie-Lynn nodded. "I *know*. That woman from the Psychic Hot Line. I've seen the commercials." When Joel only gave her a patronizing laugh, she said, "Geez, you sure didn't get much of a sense of humor when they were handing out the powers." She smiled. Then swallowed with a frown. "Please go? While I am managing to hold it all together."

With that, he turned and began walking away from her down the hallway that dead ended into a wall of lockers. The echo of each footstep grew quieter quickly as he went, and a luminescent glow came to his body, growing brighter.

Jamie-Lynn threw her head in her hands. "I can't stand watching you leave," she cried, no longer able to hold anything together.

When she looked back up, Joel Kenyan was gone.

A member of my old writing group, Nathaniel Poole, and I used to meet every Thursday at this hippie coffee joint and have what we called "write-a-thons."

We'd basically set aside four hours to write and critique a story. You had to write the story in the first three hours and then critique the other person's story in the final hour. The rule, though, was that the stories had to be complete. They had to have a beginning, middle, and an end.

You're probably thinking this resulted in a lot of really crappy stories. Actually, quite the opposite was true.

Some of my strongest short works came out of those sessions. I think it's because you're forced to not over-analyze, so you go with your gut. Two stories in particular came out of those sessions that I consider very good. This is one of them.

Love Hurts

Foster leaped naked from the tenth floor balcony of Sonya's downtown studio apartment on Euclid with a rose clenched between his teeth. Time stretched and slowed as he careened to his death and he found himself questioning his actions of late. Where had things gone wrong? Was his and Sonya's relationship really this dysfunctional? Today was their anniversary. It seemed like forever ago when they first met. The deck chairs and barbecue of Danny Logan in apartment 807 streaked past him in a blur, and Foster's thoughts drifted back to that day at the Eaton's makeup counter where Sonya was working over the holidays.

"What can I help you with?" she had asked. She was slightly taller than Foster (although Foster would find out later that the floor behind the counter was raised eight inches), with shoulder length dirty blonde hair that tied into a pair of pigtails.

"I'm looking for something to get my mom for Christmas," he had said, instantly regretting the statement. It made him sound like he was twelve instead of twenty-five. He tried to recover by adding, "I don't live with her or anything."

"Okay . . . " Sonya said, somewhat dubiously. "Well, what does she like?"

"I don't know," Foster stammered. "What do—what does *your* mom like?" Sonya wore a tight blue T-shirt that accentuated the curves of her breasts. The bottom of a tattoo peeked from below her left arm sleeve. Foster found her captivating.

She shrugged. "Perfume, maybe?"

Foster nodded. "Sure." At this point, Foster was ready to buy absolutely anything the girl suggested.

"How much do you want to spend?" Sonya asked.

"Doesn't matter," Foster said, then he worried it sounded like he didn't really care about the gift and just wanted to get the whole process over with, which wasn't what he'd meant at all. So, he added, "I mean, it's not that I don't care, it's just that money isn't an issue."

"Oh," Sonya laughed. "In that case, maybe you should take *me* shopping with you."

Foster hesitated, unsure of how to take her remark. His pulse raced and he decided he had said the right thing, whether she was joking or not. It made her laugh and a *Cosmopolitan* article he had read while waiting at the dentist had rated *He Makes Me Laugh* as the number one reason for Staying With My Man.

"What do you think of this?" Sonya asked and sprayed the inside of her wrist. She held it out for Foster to smell. He wanted to kiss it, to take her fingers into his mouth and suck on them one by one and then all at once, but he didn't.

He just sniffed and said, "I like that. I'll take it."

Sonya smiled. "That was easy."

Foster gave her his credit card and she rang in the purchase. A minute later, when she handed him his bag over the counter, he put his hand over hers on the bag, but didn't pull it toward him. "I'm Foster, by the way," he said.

"I'm Sonya," she replied, a little surprised that his hand was touching hers. *He's Confident and Assertive* had been number two on the *Cosmopolitan* list. "Thanks for shopping at Eaton's!"

"Want to go shopping with me?" he asked.

She laughed again. In his head, Foster was high fiving himself over an open issue of *Cosmo*. But she didn't answer yes or no.

"Can I give you my number?" Foster asked.

Sonya hesitated then said, "Sure." She seemed relieved that Foster finally took the bag and returned her hand to her. He asked her for a pen and some paper, and wrote his number for her. She kept glancing at the lineup of people slowly growing behind Foster who were waiting to get to the till. Her look made Foster think that she was annoyed with them, that she wished she had more time to spend talking to him. But she didn't, so Foster gave her the number and said good-bye.

He stopped before leaving the store and turned back, staring at her until she finally looked up. When she did he mimicked a telephone with the thumb and pinky of his right hand and mouthed "Call me!" the way he'd seen them do on television. She quickly turned back to her customer.

But she'd gotten the message.

Foster practically skipped home. Walking on the wings of love.

He could not believe how much of a relief it was to finally be back in the love game once again. After that last disaster, Foster worried he might be headed down the road to priesthood. His luck with women just seemed to grow more and more sour with each relationship. When Lisa ended it, he was ready to dig himself a shallow grave and tumble into it, pronouncing himself dead of a broken heart.

Was it worth it? Would it ever be worth going through that again? He didn't think so, and *One Is The Loneliest Number*, but, when his eyes met Sonya's that evening at Eaton's, Foster knew *The Power of Love* and that, ultimately, *Love Will Keep Us Together*.

And, of course, that *Love Is All You Need*.

But then he also remembered *Love Hurts*.

It hurt like a son of a bitch actually, especially when that fucker Troy knocked out four of Foster's teeth with a baseball bat. How long had Troy and Lisa been seeing each other, anyway? Foster didn't know. They seemed pretty friendly when Lisa introduced Foster as, "That creep who's been stalking me for two fucking weeks." Foster still missed the hell out of her, and maybe Sonya could help him get past that pain.

Foster liked to believe everything happened for a reason—that you could learn something from even the bad experiences—and he had definitely learned something from his relationship with Lisa. Getting his teeth knocked out had been a real eye opener, and, if it wasn't for that trip to the dentist, he would never have seen the *Cosmopolitan* article listing those ten big important reasons for Staying With My Man.

Incidentally, *His Great Smile* was number ten.

Foster ran his tongue across the four new teeth at the front of his mouth and smiled.

Three days later, Sonya still hadn't called and Foster was a wreck. He didn't dare leave his house in case the phone rang, and he hadn't slept much because there was no phone in the bedroom. So he spent his nights in the kitchen, sitting at the table on an uncomfortable wooden chair, with his head in his arms. His ass was starting to hurt, and he worried his hemorrhoids might be coming back.

The same issue of *Cosmopolitan* that had listed the reasons for Staying With My Man also had an article on dating in the new millennium. It had said that three days was the proper gestation period for women to wait before calling after meeting someone for the first time. Well, if it worked one way around, it probably worked the other way, too. So, Foster decided things had gone on long enough. It was time to take matters into his own hands and go see Sonya again.

Foster lived two and one-third miles from the mall where Sonya worked, and, by the time he shaved his face, brushed his teeth, picked out appropriate clothing, and fussed over what cologne to wear, he had to run almost the entire way in order to get there before the stores all closed

He actually didn't make it, but he got lucky. He reached the mall parking lot just in time to see Sonya walking to her car: a little blue Toyota.

Foster jogged up beside her, out of breath. "Hi! Remember me?" he asked, wheezing as he tried to naturally fall into step with her.

She looked at him wide-eyed and frightened.

"Sorry about that," Foster said, "I didn't mean to scare you." He must be a lot more stealthy than he thought. She obviously didn't hear him approaching out of the darkness.

"Hi," Sonya said. She sounded nervous. That was good. It meant she liked him.

"So, you didn't call. Or maybe you did, I might have been in the washroom. Or flossing. Did you? Call me, I mean?"

"No," she said. She started walking faster toward her car and was fumbling with her keys. Foster figured she was probably cold. It was a damn cold night. When either of them spoke, their breath hung in the air, mingling like lovers.

They got to her car and she opened the door and got inside. Foster tried to make the air phone gesture with his hand and mouth again. "Call me!" he said, but she didn't see him, and his words were cut off by the closing of her car door.

"Okay," Foster said, watching her taillights go red and slowly get smaller as she drove away, leaving him standing there waving, cold in the empty mall parking lot.

"Bye then," he said quietly to himself. "Talk to you soon."

For a minute, Foster found himself downhearted, but then he remembered reason number nine on the *Cosmopolitan* list: *He Puts Up With My Silly Moods.*

The next day, Foster awoke with one of his great ideas.

He paid a taxi cab driver to follow Sonya home that night.

He needed her address if he was going to properly woo her according to the *Cosmo* list. It cost him forty-five dollars, but he found out where she lived—in a tall apartment building on Euclid above a row of retail outlets. There was a market, a video store, a liquor store, and a pawn shop along the roadside below. Sonya parked on the street beside the building, and walked around to the front entrance. Discreetly, Foster followed behind her.

"Evening Martin," she said, walking past the grocer. He was bringing in tables of fruits and vegetables from the sidewalk below the green awning above his store.

"Evening Ms. Timms," he replied.

Then Sonya disappeared into the apartment building. Foster watched through the glass door as she got into the elevator and the doors slid closed behind her. He watched the floor light above the lift go all the way up to ten. Then he checked the tenant board beside the front door. Sure enough, there was a TIMMS listed on the tenth floor. In apartment number 1007, to be exact.

It cost Foster another twenty-five dollars for the taxi back home, but that didn't matter. Money didn't matter when you were in love.

That wasn't on the *Cosmo* list at the dentist, but Foster figured it really should have been.

Over the next two days, Foster had exactly one hundred and forty-four roses delivered to Sonya's apartment.

Surprises Me With Roses was number five on the *Cosmo* list.

They were sent in batches, and each batch came with a card. For the first day, Foster had the cards simply say things like "From a Secret Admirer" and "Thinking Of You". For the deliveries made on the next day, he decided to kick it up a notch and went with things like "Call Me—From Foster."

But Sonya didn't call. She didn't even say thank you. She was playing hard to get.

After the roses, it was time to take things to the next level. Number four on the *Cosmo* list was: *He's Playful; A*

Crazy Romantic, so Foster thought he'd give her the biggest surprise yet.

He broke into her apartment, took off all his clothes, and lay naked on her sofa on a bed of rose petals waiting for her to come home from work. He left a single rose captured seductively between his lips.

Surely, this would melt her heart, Foster thought.

But just like what happened with Lisa and Troy, Foster thought wrong.

Sonya showed up after work with Keith, a tall muscular man whom she claimed to be her fiancé. Foster recognized the look on Keith's face immediately—Keith was trying to find a baseball bat.

A *fiancé?* How could Sonya have a fiancé? There was no ring on her finger. Foster made her *laugh.* She *loved* Foster. He loved *her.* This could *not* be happening. She was Lisa all over again.

No. No! Tears filled Foster's eyes and streamed down his cheeks. *He's Not Afraid to Cry in Front of Me* had been number three on the *Cosmo* list, but it didn't matter anymore. Foster's hopes and dreams lay vanquished at his feet. Indeed, his reason for living had been quashed at the hands of this siren. If he couldn't have Sonya, life wasn't worth living.

He slid her glass door open and threw himself over the balcony, the rose still in his mouth. A split second ago, Danny Logan's barbecue had streamed past him in a blur.

So where *did* Foster go wrong? He couldn't figure it out. He'd done everything right, as far as he could tell.

Maybe he just didn't understand women. Maybe he never would. Maybe he should second think that priesthood thing after all.

His shoulder caught the edge of the fire escape on the third floor and started him spinning. His lower back bounced painfully off the railing from the second floor balcony and then the his head smashed into something on the first floor and Foster lost consciousness.

It surprised him when he woke up alive. Something wet and sticky was stinging his eyes. At first he thought it was blood, but he realized quickly it was orange juice. He had fallen through Miller Market's green awning and landed on the table of Japanese oranges.

He could see red and white flashing lights reflecting off the building through the aluminum frame of the awning, now uncovered where he had torn through.

A voice spoke to him. "Can you hear me, sir?" It was a woman—a medic from the ambulance parked on the street. Foster looked into her brown eyes. They were dotted with green flecks. "Yes," his voice wheezed out.

"Do you know what day it is today?" she asked.

Yes, of course he did—it was his and Sonya's anniversary. They had met one week ago this very day, and fallen in love at the Eaton's makeup counter. Foster stopped thinking about Sonya, and focused on the exquisite arc of the eyebrows of the woman leaning over him.

"December 16th," he groaned, his voice barely audible. Pain streaked up his spine when he spoke.

He noticed how pink and beautiful her lips were in the cold winter morning, the sweet peppermint smell on her breath. Her light brown skin was radiant.

"Can you tell me your name?" she asked.

"Foster," he said. He tried to sit up, to ask hers. But she held him down with a soft, loving hand.

"Please don't try to move, sir. Your arms and legs are broken, and possibly your back. We're going to move you to a gurney and take you to the hospital."

Foster closed his eyes.

"Foster," the woman called out, her voice like Christmas bells. "Stay with me Foster. Keep your eyes open. Do you understand? I need you to stay with me." He opened his eyes and looked into hers again.

"You still there, Foster?" she asked.

"Yes," he said. More pain shot through him. He tried to say more but could only get out a whisper.

"What was that, honey?" she asked, leaning forward, putting her ear inches from his lips. She smelled clean. And pretty.

"What's your name?" he asked, enduring the pain.

She smiled. "Rebecca. You stay with me now Foster, okay?" *He needs me more than I need him.* That was number six, or maybe it had been number seven on the *Cosmo* list. Foster couldn't really remember anymore.

He smiled back. He wasn't going anywhere. He was in love.

He just wished he still had the rose in his mouth.

I originally wrote **The Reality of Time** *for a DAW anthology called* Swordplay, *but it ended up too long. Then I realized I was almost out of time to submit a story. I needed another one fast. I came away with this, and, in many ways, I like it more than the other one.*

Ultimately, it didn't matter. DAW didn't use either story. They said Fallen *was far too shocking to their sensitive readership. At the same time, Denise Little, the editor of the anthology, told me it was probably an award-winning story — it just needed the right market.*

Well, things have gotten in the way, like they always do, and Fallen *has sat alone on my hard drive just waiting to shock some sensitive readers . . .*

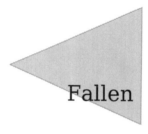

Fallen

Sagami Province, Japan, 1560

Sengo Suramasa challenged his master, Goro Nyudo Masamune, in a contest to prove Japan's greatest swordsmith.

Exactly one year later, they met where the split creek narrowed to one.

Suramasa arrived first. His beard hung down the center of his kimono. Blood red, it matched the grip of the sword in his hand: Juuchi Fuyu; Ten Thousand Winters, his greatest work. He spotted Masamune walking with difficulty up the grassy hill and smiled thinly. No longer the great legend of Japan, the old man moved slowly now, while time continued to move fast. After today, Suramasa would become the legend.

When Masamune finally got close, Suramasa bowed slightly. "Hello old friend," he said jokingly. "I started thinking you might not show up."

"Oh Suramasa, you know better than that," he said, his voice as dry and brittle as he.

Nodding at the hilt protruding from his old master's sheath, Suramasa asked, "Do you have faith in your work?"

"Aye," Masamune answered quietly.

"What is the name?"

"Yawraaka-Te." Tender Hands.

Suramasa held back a smile. Even the old man's swords no longer sounded menacing. He held up his own, admiring the blade. "Behold Juuchi Fuyu! My greatest work."

"Aye." With a leathery hand, Masamune motioned to the creek. "Proceed."

Suramasa strutted to the water's edge. On this hill, the creek flowed quickly. He held Juuchi Fuyu to the sky. Then, with a final look to Masamune, plunged the blade straight down into the water's depths, facing the sharpened edge against the current.

Everything flowing down the creek, the smallest fish, the most delicate plum blossom, the most rusted leaf, even the very air riding above the water, was sliced cleanly in two by Suramasa's perfect blade. He grinned up at his old master. "You see?" he said. "My finest work!"

Masamune nodded. "It is indeed. I am most impressed."

Satisfied, Suramasa lifted his blade from the current and proudly held it dripping in the sharp light of the afternoon sun before wiping it and returning it to its sheath. "Your turn, old friend."

Slowly, Masamune made his way to the water. Suramasa watched, wondering if perhaps the old man might stumble and fall in. Farther upstream, before the split became one, a waterwheel creaked, spinning against the side of a chocolate brown shed. A burst of warm wind picked plum blossoms from the trees behind it, littering them across the grass and water. Finally, Masamune reached the creek. Slowly, he unsheathed his sword, bent at the waist, and gently lowered his blade into the water.

Suramasa watched him stand there, motionless, while his sword cut nothing coming down the stream. Not a fish. Not a flower. Not even a single leaf. Everything swept safely around the blade. Suramasa saw a guppy swim up, touch the edge of the blade with its nose, and swim away. He could no longer hold back his laugher. "You have made the opposite of a fine sword!" he bellowed. "Your sword cuts nothing!"

Masamune brought the blade from the water, wiped it dry, and slid it back into its sheath. "Aye." Slowly, he straightened, and Suramasa saw him smiling.

"What are you so happy about, old man? You lost!"

Masamune's attention was fixed on a monk making his way down the rolling hill from the direction of the waterwheel, the sun beaming from his bald head. He wore saffron and crimson robes, and his feet were clad in sandals. He smiled at the swordsmiths.

"I saw your contest," he explained. "I wish to give you my account of what I witnessed."

Suramasa laughed. "Yes, yes. Please do." With a sweep of his hand, he gestured for the monk to continue.

"The first sword," the monk said, nodding to Suramasa, "your sword. It is a fine, fine sword. By all accounts, a sword of perfection." The wind picked up, showering pink blossoms across the robin's egg sky behind him.

Grinning, Suramasa nodded agreement.

"However," the monk continued, "it is bloodthirsty. It cuts everything in its path, without consideration or conscience. It is the embodiment of evil. It will slice children as easily as kite string." The monk placed his hand on Masamune's shoulder. "Your sword made not a single unnecessary cut. Unequivocally, it is the finer blade, bestowing mercy on the innocent and undeserving."

"Aye," Masamune said.

Nodding to both men, the monk headed back, following the creek.

Without a glance to Suramasa, Masamune started down the hill, his steps slow, careful and feeble.

Suramasa watched, feeling the tides of unbalance in his mind, and the weight of the sword called Ten Thousand Winters sheathed at his side. Pulling out the blade, he looked at it one final time with disgust before tossing it angrily into the creek.

He trudged away.

Down below its clear depths, the creek's current tugged at the blood-thirsty sword, finally lifting it from the smooth stones lining its bottom. It carried the weapon along its twisted path, following the flow of water, and slipping through the flow of time.

Vancouver, British Columbia, Canada — Today

Patient: B.Dawson/1
Rcv: 6/January

This is my journal, as requested by Dr. Payne (which, if you ask me, is a great name for a James Bond villain, but a ridiculous name for a real doctor. But hey, he seems to do all right, so what do I know?). I suppose I should start this first entry explaining why this journal even exists.

To me, it's rather pointless because I already blog at least once a day (www.baileydawson.com, in case you're interested).

"That one's public," the good doc explained. "This one will only be seen by you and me."

Okay, maybe he's a pretty good shrink and that, but if he read my online stuff at all, I think he'd realize I don't hold much back. It's not really my style. And besides, I don't buy into this whole "just you and me" thing. Having already achieved a modicum of success with my graphic novels, and having no immediate plans to do anything but become even more wildly successful, these journals will be published one day. You know, just like Sylvia Plath's were. This is why I'm referring to you in the third person, Dr. Payne, because reading stuff in the second person makes you feel like Sybil. This way, it'll be easier for people twenty years from now, after I gas myself with an oven, or strangle myself in an automatic towel dispenser while masturbating.

Just in case it's not clear, that was a joke. Seriously. I'm not nearly as crazy as Sylvia. Or Michael Hutchence.

There's one weird rule, too. I have to submit each section as I finish. He promises he'll return them to me later on. In return, I had to promise not to keep any copies. I guess I'm not supposed to know what I've already written, which is another thing that makes no sense. But hey, I'm the one seeing the shrink, so what do I know? I'm the one who's nutso.

Okay, the writer in me is starting to twitch because, as far as storytelling goes? So far this thing's Snoozeville. Let's see if I can fix that (she says, briskly rubbing her hands together).

Ahem.

The pills get away from me sometimes, and I actually get scared.

There, I said it.

The Dex, I mean. The others aren't an issue, but the Dex? I could take a whole month's prescription worth over three days and wish I had another month to start into after that.

This is why I finally broke down and asked Kent (he's my boyfriend) to regulate them for me. We agreed to him dishing them out a week's worth at a time. This way, inside of that week, I can still over-medicate to a certain degree, but not so much that, you know, I turn into a teenage pop star gone nutso or anything.

So, what's wrong with me: I have type II bipolar disorder and ADHD topped with a light sprinkle of OCD for flavor. I'm told these three often come packaged together.

To balance me out, every day I take 1500mg divalproex sodium (a mood stabilizer which is really anti-seizure medication—don't ask me how these things work), 4mg clonazepam (an anti-anxiety drug), and I'm supposed to take 20mg of Dexedrine (a systemic amphetamine). The Dexedrine produces dopamine in my attention-challenged brain, allowing me to focus enough to get my writing done. Problem is, it works extremely well. The more I take, the more I write. I have literally stayed awake three days straight and written fifty-thousand words, almost without leaving my seat. And I know what you're thinking, but you're wrong. Four days later, when I finally wake up, it's actually pretty damn good writing. It's paying my bills, let's just say that.

Probably one day my heart will just explode, but I don't play sports, or bungee jump, or leap out of airplanes, so I just chalk this up to my way of living on the edge.

I write a graphic novel called *Fallen*. You might have heard of it. I actually have a big readership. There's fan pages on the net and everything. Last year at Comic-Con in San Diego? I signed books for two hours straight, nonstop. Of course, it helped that right before the room opened, I gave Neil Gaiman the first two *Fallen* trade paperbacks and he left them sitting on his table. Nothing like having Neil silently support your efforts to gain a fan base.

I love Neil. Apparently it shows in my work. I gets lots of emails asking if *Sandman* inspired *Fallen* at all. *Duh*. I think *Sandman* inspired every comic that followed it, the way Shakespeare inspired all writers to come. Neil Gaiman, Alan Moore, and Frank Miller—they're the Shakespeares and Dantes of the panel-story world. I should put that on a T-shirt.

Fallen tells the story of Mist, a fallen Valkyrja who got booted out of Asgaard for complaining too much. Oh, she had enjoyed the "swooping over battlefields with her sisters on squadrons of winged wolves, picking through the souls of the dead looking for heroes" part. But the rest of the job? The "being handmaiden to Odin's ill-mannered and ungrateful army sitting slovenly around Valhalla waiting for Ragnarök part"? Or the "serving up booze and boar Sæhrímnir while being drunkenly ass-slapped" part? That all sucked. And, by far, the majority of her time was spent being ass-slapped. Eventually, Mist complained about it too much, and Brynhildr took her aside and gently suggested maybe she should hit the curb.

So, in *Fallen*, Mist and her white steed, Hawk, forbidden to ever return to Asgaard, adventure throughout Scandinavia (and occasionally other parts of Europe), searching for living heroes while struggling against miscellaneous forces of darkness.

That's it, in a nutshell. The real comic's a lot darker than I make it sound here. The mythology's pretty accurate, though. Usually, anyway. Although I try to avoid the Norse pantheon's deep-rooted predilection for incest (they had this really creepy thing for "relations with relations"). I take other liberties, too, but there's tons of stuff lost in history from those mythos, so I don't feel too badly about it. Sometimes, I'll even throw stuff in that's completely outside the realm of Norse mythology. The story I'm writing now is like that. It's a six issue arc involving a sixteenth century Japanese sword. And yeah, that makes all kinds of no sense, but ultimately the story's the most important part.

So that's what I do. I'm Bailey Dawson, and I write comics.

Okay, time to drop another bomb. And, just like my secret about turning into Charlie Sheen with my Dex? This is another thing nobody knows.

I'm pregnant.

Yep, just five months out of high school and look at me! I've already ruined my life.

I haven't even told Kent yet. And yes, I know, his name's so lame. But once you get past that part of him, he's actually quite cool. We live in my parents' basement, which also sounds lame, but again, once you get past it, it's also kind of cool of them to let us stay there.

They will especially flip when they find out I'm preggers. Kent's gonna flip, too, but not nearly as much as my folks. Kent's pretty stable (thank God). He's my rock.

I'm actually writing this right now while sitting on a bus headed to the doctor (a real one, not my shrink) to verify what the little purple stick I peed on told me. But those things are like, what? 99.99999% accurate, right? So I have no great hope I somehow messed up the procedure and got it wrong, or anything like that. I'm guessing I'm probably two months along or so.

It's freezing cold on this bus. It doesn't help that my window is jammed open an inch and I can't push it closed. I should just move seats, but I'm too lazy. Not like there aren't lots to choose from, I'm the only passenger onboard. Wouldn't matter anyway, I've felt cold for weeks. Must have something to do with my new found condition. Even though it's fall, it feels like winter. It's felt like winter for ages. Outside it even *looks* like winter; everything's so cold, stark, and dead.

Maybe I'm just being negative.

Hey, that's weird.

A poem just popped into my head. I think my mom used to recite it to me when I was a baby. Or maybe not. I don't recall ever remembering it before now.

Cherry blossom, cherry blossom
      Pumpkin Pie.
  Water falls, big beach balls
Please don't cry.
     Moonlit nights, moonlit nights
       Fairy Queens.
  You can trust the magic dust
Just go on and dream.

She told me . . .

    I was . . . when . . .

She called me Pumpkin.

Pie . . .

    . . .a baby.

Patient: B.Dawson/2
Rcv: 9/January

I'm in the hospital.

The bus I was on was in an accident. Something totally rammed into the side of it. I'm not really sure what happened, but whatever it was, it was big, it came fast, and it hit hard. I remember feeling the slam, then being knocked across the aisle. My head careened off the metal side of the seat beside me and I tumbled onto the floor. I also remember hearing that sick squeak of metal like you hear in submarine movies, and the bus began toppling sideways. I started sliding, thinking, *Shit, it's going right over*, but somehow it didn't. It came crashing back onto its wheels instead. My head pounded like a son of a bitch, but at least I was alive. It happened so fast, I didn't even really have time to be scared or even react. Then, the next thing I remember was not being able to move my arms. No matter how hard I tried to lift them, they just stayed limp at my side. I panicked, my heart raced, and then . . . nothing.

I don't remember anything after that until I woke up here.

Here is a bright, white, and clean hospital room. I was confused, but after my real-life reenactment of *The Sweet Hereafter*? Very much happy to be alive, thank you.

When I came to, I still couldn't move my arms. I started flipping again until I realized I could move my fingers. So I laid there, staring at the lights, making my fingers do little dances and thinking, *If I can move them, things can't be too bad, can they?*

I must stop here and explain something. I believe all of us have a thread of rationality inside our head that never shuts down, no matter what. Timothy Leary could throw a suitcase of pharmaceuticals at it, and it might duck and cover, but it will still be there, making sure that even when we're messed up, we're not truly, truly messed up. Do you know what I mean? It's the thing separating us from the droolers.

I tell you this because it was that thin thread of rationality that noticed something wasn't quite right with me lying there enjoying my finger dance like it was the *Vagina Monologues* or something. It pondered this, eventually deciding there could be only one explanation: They had me on happy pills. And, looking at my arms, I discovered the reason I couldn't lift them had less to do with my bus accident and more to do with the straps tying them down to the bars on the side of my bed.

Yep, you know what that meant. Holy macaroni cannelloni! They'd put me on the psych ward.

This slightly concerned my fiber of rationality. It has seen far too many movies where people get trapped in places like this for weeks. The rest of my brain was doing a little happy dance, celebrating that this probably meant a constant supply of happy pills for the near future.

That's when a tall guy with a round face and, like, seven pieces of curly hair on his head (making him look exactly like Charlie Brown, if Charlie Brown wore Buddy Holly glasses) came into my room carrying a sword. He wore gray sweats with a long red T that hung almost to his knees. Had it not been for the stethoscope around his neck, I'd have guessed him a fourteen-year-old mental patient escapee from another room, come to stab me to death.

"Oh, you've woken up," he said. He wore braces. *Seriously*. And in this bright room? It was like staring straight into the chrome grate of a Buick. Leaning the sword on its blade against the wall, he picked up my chart. "How are you feeling?"

My mouth was dry and icky. "I keep waiting for the Oompa Loompas," I said, bringing a cringe to my strand of rationality which now figured with a comment like that I'd probably be trapped here for months.

For some reason, at the time, I didn't find the fact that he had brought a sword strange at all. Maybe it was the pills they had me on.

Placing his stethoscope below my throat, he asked me to breathe. "Your chest sounds good."

"I have a question," I said. "On the bus, I couldn't move my arms. Now I'm here, and you've got them strapped down. Will they be unstrapped soon, so I can see if they work or not?"

"Our regulations are to restrain all new patients their first forty-eight hours." He returned my chart to the end of my bed. "In the past, we've had a few incidents. Your doctor will be here soon. He can make an assessment when he arrives."

Confused, I shook my head. "An assessment about what?"

A nurse came in and checked the bags of fluid hanging from the stand that were dripping into my wrist through an IV.

"I don't understand," I said. "I was on my way to get my first pregnancy checkup and—"

The doctor's eyebrows went up. Glancing to the nurse, he finally looked at me. "You're pregnant?"

I nodded.

"Are you sure?"

"Pretty sure."

His eyes shifted to the bags of fluid. "Take her off the benzodiazepine, the zopiclone and the fluvoxamine."

"Is this going to cause any problems?" I asked.

"No."

"Then why are you taking me off them now?"

"Just better to be safe. Listen, your doctor will be here soon. He'll be able to answer your questions better than me. TLAs aren't really my specialty. I deal mainly with schizophrenia."

"TLAs?"

"Three letter acronyms. You know, DID, BPD, OCD, ADD, DID, there's forty or so of them. Hard to keep track, really. Anyway, if Dr. Payne hasn't shown up in the next few hours, I'll come back and check on you. In the meantime, get some rest." He leaned over and I heard him whisper to the nurse to give me a pregnancy test.

"You think I'd lie about being pregnant? And *three hours*?! You can't keep me tied down like this for three hours."

Unsnapping his latex gloves, he dropped them into the biohazard container on his way to the door. "We just want to be thorough."

"Aren't you going to take your sword?" He turned, and I gestured with my chin to the back wall where he left it. It looked fancy, like the real deal. And trust me, I know my swords. My dad's a professor of archeology and mythology at Simon Fraser University; it's part of my secret to making *Fallen* as accurate as I do. Actually, this sword had a scarlet grip and black pommel like the Japanese one Mist finds in my current *Fallen* story.

He glanced at the sword then back to the nurse. "Actually," he said, "keep her on the benzo, but lower it to 10mg until you get the PT back."

I fell asleep for a bit after that. I dreamt of the sword from my story. According to legend, it could consume the minds of those it came in contact with. Maybe that's my problem! What do you think, Doc? If only things were that easy, hey?

The sword the doctor had left in my room was gone when I woke up, and, unfortunately, the happy pills had worn off. The nurse returned to tell me my psychiatrist was going to be a few more hours. I started to protest, but she interrupted. "He said it would be okay to re-move your restraints."

That's how I've been able to journal all this. Oh, and in case you haven't figured it out, my arms work now.

The nurses here are actually pretty cool. I've seen two so far, and both have been nice to me. The one who removed my restraints has mocha-colored skin, and is probably in her midthirties. The other one keeps poking her head in to make sure I don't need any more ice water or anything. She has chestnut hair, almost the same color as mine, only shorter. And hers has bounce—mine just hangs flat. She's the one who brought me this pad of foolscap and a pen. I just love words like foolscap. Writing them makes me feel like I'm in the eighteenth century or something. For the same reason, Mist is a fallen Valkyrja, not a Valkryie.

Okay, call me pretentious.

I suppose eventually I'm going to have to rewrite the first journal page I did. It didn't survive my near death bus experience.

And on that note, Dr. Payne just walked in, so I guess thus endeth this installment of my strange little journal.

Patient: B.Dawson/3
Rcv: 10/January

Dr. Payne left a few hours ago and took with him the four pages of foolscap I wrote since becoming hospitalized. He told me not to worry about rewriting the stuff I lost on the bus. He said it's more important to focus on the present.

Well, presently, I am still in hospital, and still unsure why, exactly, it's the psych ward they've got me on. Dr. Payne told me not to be concerned about it, but he didn't really explain it, either.

"How long'll I be here?" I asked.

"Couple days, Bailey. We just want to keep an eye on you."

"What about my parents?"

"I've talked to them, don't worry."

"How about Kent? Can he come visit?"

Dr. Payne glanced away uncomfortably. "It's better if you don't have visitors right now, okay? Consider this a vacation. Time to relax."

I explained I had a comic book in need of finishing, but he assured me again I'd be home in a few days.

"You said a couple days a minute ago. Now it's a few?" See, I'm naturally paranoid.

"Two or three."

"Three is fifty percent bigger than two. That's substantial."

He smiled. "You'll be out soon, I promise. Can't you do your writing here?"

Well sure, but that isn't the point. It's all those movies where people get trapped in places like this.

"I'll be back tomorrow. In the meantime, Dr. Glasgow will look after you." He patted my leg. "You're on vacation."

Truth is, I'm not that worried about *Fallen*. I'm actually five months ahead on it. The latest issue on the shelf is number two of an eight issue story called *Passing*

Seasons, and the publisher got the whole kit and caboodle a month ago.

It's good, too. Mist and Hawk find Freyr's magic sword, the one that can fight by itself.

For those of you not geeky enough to know your Norse mythology, during a trip to Niflheim (the underworld), Freyr gets the hotness for this giantess named Gerðr. Although he's the god of all things goodness, I'm guessing Freyr's a bit light in the looks department because he has to send Skimir, his faithful messenger, to woo Gerðr, and she only agrees to marry him after Skimir threatens her life with Freyr's sword, which inexplicably gets lost afterwards.

Passing Seasons begins in issue twenty-eight of *Fallen*. Mist discovers Freyr's sword while returning from a visit with Loki in Niflheim. The story climaxes in *Fallen* thirty-five when Mist uses it to save the Valkyrja Fray (Mist's best friend from Asgaard) from Jörmungandr, the world serpent. Afterwards, the sword is lost in the depths of the sea. This is important because eventually the fire giant Surtr must find it so he can, with absolute perfect irony, use it to kill an unarmed Freyr during Ragnarök.

When I finally decide to stop writing *Fallen* (and, like Neil did with *Sandman*, I'll do it while it's still popular), I plan to end on a twelve issue Ragnarök story. The Norse mythos is full of coolness, but Ragnarök is the bomb. That whole Christian Apocalypse with the horsemen and Satan and everything? It's Mardis Gras compared to Ragnarök.

Ragnarök pits Odin and his army of heroic souls against the underworld in the ultimate battle. The planet trembles. Trees tear from the soil roots and all. Tsunamis ravage the planet. Loki rises with a ship full of the great army of the dead. Fire giants tear apart the skies. Mountains crack open releasing hordes of troll-wives. It's a bloodbath ending with the destruction of Earth.

It'd be hard to continue the series if I changed my mind after those issues hit the shelves.

Anyway, I have no immediate plans to quit. I'm enjoying Mist's adventures too much right now.

Man, whatever they're pumping into me through this IV is making me sleepy. Think I'll have a little lie down.

Patient: B.Dawson/4
Rcv: 11/January

Day two here at Psycho World. Dr. Payne just left.

"How's the vacation?" he asked.

"Lacking a beach and the food isn't exactly five star."

He smiled. "Charlie Brown been checking on you from time to time?"

It took a minute to figure out what he meant. "Oh," I said, "so you actually *read* the stuff I write?"

"Of course, I wouldn't ask for it otherwise. And you're very entertaining. Most of my patients lull me into comas, but your journal's great. I even learn new things."

I held out what I wrote yesterday. "Here, have some more. Learn away."

"Can you bring me some *Fallen* to read during our next session?"

Surprised, I smiled. "Hell ya! I'll even sign 'em. 'From your craziest patient, Bailey.' "

"You're not my craziest. Not by far."

I leaned forward, suddenly curious. "Tell me about the craziest," I said, lowering my voice.

"I can't. Sorry," he said with a chuckle. "Anyway, I was wondering, since today would normally be our weekly session, would you mind if we continued your therapy here?"

I shrugged. "Sure."

He locked the door, turned off the lights, and closed the blinds. The hypnosis and regression thing lasted about an hour. Afterward, he switched the lights back on and checked my chart. "You've had a few blood tests, I see."

"Yeah, with all the needles being stuck in me, I'm starting to feel like Courtney Love."

"Everything looks good. I think we'll send you home tomorrow."

Hooray. Back to *Fallen*.

The story I'm working on now, *Winter of Destruction*, arcs over six issues. It involves the sixteenth century Japanese sword I told you about, flung back to the time of the Vikings. It's based on an actual sword the archeology department at my dad's university received a couple months ago to study. For two days, he brought it home so I could sketch, photograph, and use it for reference. Part of what makes *Fallen* special, I think, is that my dad inspires me with new stuff all the time. The minute I held that sword, I knew it would be in the next story. It felt powerful. Heavy. It made you want to just go out and start swinging it around. The hilt was gorgeous—a gold guard, a deep red grip and a pommel that looked like an eight-ball.

It even has a kick-ass name: Juuchi Fuyu or, in English, Ten Thousand Winters. Sengo Suramasa, considered it his greatest work.

Suramasa was Japan's second-best swordsmith. He was also evil, crazy, and bloodthirsty. According to legend, so were his swords. When people susceptible to their power wielded a Suramasa sword, a dark evil crept into their minds and wouldn't leave until blood had been drawn by the blade in their hands. Sometimes, that blood turned out to be their own.

Lately, I've been having recurring dreams about the sword, sometimes very dark ones. But then, my work does tend to consume me until its finished.

In *Winter of Destruction*, Þráinn, the Draugar witch-king (a sort of undead vampire thing), has plunged Scandinavia into an endless winter. Mist kills him with Juuchi Fuyu. She then forsakes the Suramasa sword in favor of Mistletoe—Þráinn's sword—which segues into the next story.

See how easy this is? The writing's always been simple for me. It's the drawing that takes the time.

Patient: B.Dawson/5
Rcv: 17/January

Home again. Jiggety-jig.

It's almost three in the afternoon. I had to wait for Dr. Payne to come and release me. Apparently Charlie Brown didn't have the authority. I called Kent, but he didn't answer, so Mom picked me up. Dr. Payne asked me to give her my journal pages each day and let her keep them until our next session, like I'm a six-year-old or something.

Mom acted weird all the way home. No idea why. I guess having your kid go to the nuthouse for a couple days does that to you.

I wouldn't know. I never . . .

Weird.

I suddenly feel . . .

Wait.

Whoa. That was weird.

I just puked. Like harsh. Twenty-five minutes at the toilet harsh. It was disgusting. Now my stomach feels like a Cirque du Soleil stage in the middle of act 2.

I'm gonna go lie down.

Patient: B.Dawson/6
Rcv: 17/January

So, when I got home yesterday, Kent was gone. Splitsville. No note, no nothing. Took all his stuff.

Like, hello? I asked my parents, but, as usual, they were clueless. Or they didn't want to talk about it. One or the other.

Whatever.

I'm getting a bit sick of the kindergarten treatment. Apparently Dr. Payne put Mom in charge of my meds, which harshly bites because now I can't even do the "abuse just a week's worth at a time" thing like I did with Kent.

Anyway, I'm gonna finish my first draft of the *Winter* script and go to bed.

Patient: B.Dawson/7
Rcv: 17/January

Been a strange couple days. Haven't been journaling. Sorry, don't kill me for it.

Not sure what's going on, but I keep tossing chunks into the toilet, and I'm dizzy all the time. Everything will be fine one minute and then something in my head just snaps and it all changes.

It's like being run down by a locomotive full of badness.

I'm almost done laying out the panels for all six issues of *Winter*. Generally, I like to pencil the whole arc from start to finish, and then complete everything else (the inking, word balloons, all that other crap) one comic at a time. *Fallen*'s a black and white comic (other than the cover). I do the covers last, and someone else colors them.

Sera, my editor at Black Rose Comics, likes getting my work one issue at a time, anyway. Sera completely kicks ass. She's probably the single coolest chick ever. If I was a lesbo? I'd totally dyke out with Sera.

Patient: B.Dawson/8
Rcv: 17/January

Spent most of yesterday and today in bed. I can't face the world or even be awake for it. I'm not even sure why. My stomach's bloated with this horrible dread that sloshes around but won't leave. I'm feel like that whiney chick who wrote *Prozac Nation*. By the end of that book I was so sick of her I wished she'd just slit her wrists.

That's how I feel.

Not good, I know.

I can't even write. Thinking about Suramasa's bloodthirsty sword twists my stomach into knots. And when I sleep, it appears in my dreams along with other nightmarish things so vividly . . . but I can't even begin to describe them. Trying to makes my stomach clench.

Shit . . .

I'm back. I can't keep puking like this, can I?

Thank God I have a session with Dr. Payne tomorrow.

Dr. Payne returned my journal entries today. I guess that's a good sign?

I feel more messed up than ever, though. We had a long session today. Three hours. Halfway through, I broke down and, I don't know how to explain it . . . something busted apart inside me. Whatever I had built to hide everything away, toppled down and everything rushed out, bringing with it a weird combination of relief and despair.

Even now, I have to keep stopping to cry, or get up and walk around to keep from focusing on any one thing for too long. Just randomly, emotions quickly sweep through me, completely overwhelming, and, yet, indescribable.

And now I know why all of this happened. Because today I learned the truth.

Today I remembered all the puzzle pieces my brain had tried to tuck away from me and block out of existence. It's amazing what your survival instinct is capable of.

No wonder my mind decided it best to just not have to cope with all this. Instead, it traveled back in time almost exactly one year.

Back to when Kent was still here.

And Cody was still here. Or on his way, anyway.

Shit. Here come the tears. Just thinking his name makes me sob uncontrollably. How is it that a week ago I didn't even remember him being born, yet now I can recall every second of the five months we were together as though they were happening right now.

I can see him. I can hear him.

Oh God.

I can smell him.

I can smell him.

Then there's the day everything changed. I will never forget that. Not again. No matter how many pills I throw at it, that one's gonna be with me to the grave.

It hurts so much to think about, I'm worried I might go back to drinking.

Cody was sitting in his blue bath seat. I had filled the bathtub to his chest. He liked baths. He always slapped the top of the water and laughed. So much joy. Cody was such a happy baby.

But not me. For weeks, I'd been bitter and angry, quick to temper. Every day it worsened. Kent noticed it. Christ, even I noticed it. But that didn't help.

It started just after dad brought that sword home. Juuchi Fuyu: Ten Thousand Winters. But that could have nothing to do with any of this. That's just my natural paranoia at work.

Kent kept trying to help. "What's wrong?" he'd say.

I resented him more and more each time he asked.

Dr. Payne thinks I suffered from post-partum depression.

Whatever it was, the feelings grew darker and deeper.

That is, until that morning with Cody. He sat there in the tub, so trusting. Smiling, laughing, and splashing. Trusting me. His mother.

Going through the motions of washing him, I begrudged the world's happiness.

With a squeal, Cody splashed both hands and smiled at me.

Something sprung loose in my head.

I toppled his bath seat backward. His face slipped under the water. Silence gathered. I felt relief.

He was too little to know what was happening, too young to climb up out of the seat. At first, he looked calm. Then, that was replaced by surprised. Then panic gripped him. Flailing beneath the water, his wide blue eyes stared desperately to mine, pleading for mommy to save him.

But Mommy didn't save him. Mommy watched him drown.

I told the police I'd stepped out less than a minute. Just long enough to grab a towel.

They reported Cody's death accidental.

Kent didn't believe it, though. Within a week, he moved out, and I started going nuts with my meds again. My parents called Dr. Payne and I started seeing him weekly. He suggested the hypnosis and regression therapy, and asked me to keep this journal.

You know the rest. Probably better than I do.

It's funny, I don't remember writing the early journals. There was no bus. I was here, at my easel, swallowing a month's worth of Dexedrine and clonazepam.

Although Dr. Payne said it's no longer needed, I think I'll keep writing this journal. He was right—it's different than my blog. My blog isn't written by me, it's written by that chick who writes *Fallen*. Somehow those two people aren't the same. I'm not sure why.

Anyway, I think it's time to take a break from *Fallen*. It's grown too dark. Or maybe it's as dark as ever, and my life just needs more light right now.

I could write the final twelve issues ending it completely, but for now I think I'll just put it on hiatus and work on getting through the remainder of this winter.

Enough blood has been drawn.

I'm not ready for another Ragnarök.

This story was written for a workshop I attended with Dean Wesley Smith and Kristine Kathryn Rusch. We had to write two stories. I can't remember the theme of the other one, *but this one had to be military science fiction. I had absolutely no idea what military science fiction was.*

So I guessed.

Apparently I guessed right, because Dean told me to send it out immediately (which of course, I didn't. Authors are probably the laziest bunch of schmucks you'll ever meet).

The story was inspired by Warren Ellis's Ocean, *a graphic novel I fell in love with. Warren Ellis is a genius. My story probably doesn't reach Ellis standards, but I still think it's good.*

Nashville Beaumont

I cup the Digimate™ in my fingers, thumbing the uniball controller, flipping through requestors. They project two-dimensionally above my hand, translucent squares of near-infinite thinness, hard to see in the park's late-afternoon sunlight. I step into the shadows of the copse of pine and oak where I've hidden my pack, just outside the playground. I have a love/hate relationship with playgrounds; for me they serve only as brief sanctuaries while I plan my next move.

Then again, I only discovered playgrounds six months ago.

Today there are no children here, and that makes me wary; it makes me feel like the shiny white device in my hand tags me from miles away, even though it's hardly larger than my index finger. It's capable of projecting holos of fifty cubic centimeters, but I've got it cranked down to less than five, and the trees hide me, cutting off all angles to the road.

Even still, I feel conspicuous.

I drop through the Digimate™'s binary tree of options, selecting RECORD from the AUDIOGROUP.

.CLICK.

A breeze of pine wells up as the square selector disappears in a blink, replaced by a single horizontal line floating in its place. I clear my throat. The line follows, jetting by with zigzags, mapping the waveform. "Test. This is a test."

.REPLAY.

With perfect digital clarity, the audio plays back, accompanied by the wave.

I glance around one more time. The angles are tight. Nobody can see me. The playground is empty. A laser swing silently sways on the wind.

.RECORD.

"My name is Nashville Beaumont. I'm twelve years old. Few people know I exist. I was born in Texas." I hesitate on the word "born". Take a breath. "I have a twin sister. I don't know where she is. My plan is to find her."

The line goes flat as I consider my next words. Doesn't matter. Silence gets compressed into a single parameter of empty-time. Silence costs nothing.

Two crows swoop out of the trees, diving right behind my flattened wave, scaring me. I remember the chance I'm taking being out here in the open.

A coldness scampers up my spine.

But that's why I need some sort of diary. In case I get caught. Otherwise, this will all be for nothing.

I swallow. My lips are dry. "Her name's Providence." Closing my eyes, I sigh. "I can't remember her. If we ever met, it was long ago. Likely, we were separated at—" Here comes that uncomfortable word again, but there isn't a better one. "—birth."

.CLICK.

The Digimate™ turns off. Instantly, the holo-line disappears. Across the park a crow caws. I decide I have to finish.

.CLICK.

"I will find her," I say. "Then I will kill Kidar Frenzid." My stomach clenches at the thought of hurting anyone. Even him: the man who murdered my entire family while I watched. Confused pain shoots through my head. I shake it off. "This much I know: my name's Nashville Beaumont . . ."

" . . . and I'm a weapon."

.CLICK.

Once on the street, I feel better. There are people. I fold into the tide of them moving up the sidewalk. Here in Argentina, public traffic literally swallows you up. In the six months since I escaped from Texas, I've never felt as invisible as in the crowded streets of Argentine cities.

People walk so close, they touch. In Americanada people fear contact.

Still I have to be careful, so I make three random turns then check over my shoulder. I half expect to see that man, the one who managed to follow me across the sun-bleached Texas desert. Somehow, among that heat-pounded land of death, creosote bushes, cacti, poisonous snakes, black scorpions, and split-tongued lizards, he tracked me to Florida before I even noticed him. That scares me. I'm not as good as I think.

I managed to lose him in Northern Brazil, at least I hope I did. Still, I worry he came far enough to realize where I'm headed. Or that they've replaced him with someone else.

Behind me, two men in sunglasses round the corner. Always it's men making me suspicious—probably because of Kidar Frenzid. To be safe, I duck into a small *supermercado* and watch through the window as they stroll by, waiting for even a slight glance my way. I don't see one.

The clerk at the counter clears his throat.

I set two bottles of water on the counter and ask directions to the MagLev station. I'm fluent in seven languages, Spanish being one. My studies in the Compound started before I can remember. Despite my age, I've been told I'm better trained than many people in their chosen professions.

Instead of giving me directions, the clerk asks, "Where are you headed?"

I see no point in lying. "The seaside. Punta Tombo."

He smiles. "By yourself? Where's your mother?"

"Waiting at the flat for me to bring directions to the train."

He shakes his head. "Your mother should not take the ML. Better by bus. Half the price. At *least* half. And only one, maybe two hours longer."

"Okay."

He even knows which bus to take and the schedule. As he draws me a map, a man wearing a tan leather hat walks past the store. My heart nearly stops. It's the same man I thought I left in Brazil; he's still following me. A tangle of black hair sprouts from beneath his hat. His face is unshaven. His eyes are gray. A denim jacket almost hides a black T-shirt beneath. Our eyes meet, and he knows I recognize him. He *wants* me to recognize him. He doesn't care, and that scares me because he thinks I haven't got a chance.

I want to sprint out, grab his jacket, shake him, scream at him to leave me alone. Tell him I haven't escaped a supposed "impenetrable" underground compound—trekked through an entire continent—only to be recaptured now. But I don't. Instead, I pay the clerk, and by the time I'm back on the street, the man in the hat is gone.

"Mi amigo!" the clerk calls from inside the store. "Tell your mom they launch the rocket-shuttles to the International Space Station in Punta Tombo. She gets you there tomorrow, you might even see it!" He says it all in Spanish.

I thank him, smiling. But I already know about tomorrow's launch.

I'll be on it.

"Now hers!" Kidar Frenzid snaps. Tears stand in my mother's eyes. She can't talk, her mouth is duct-taped. The rest of the roll is in my hand. I've just finished taping her, and my father, sister, and brother to our kitchen chairs. Kidar Frenzid brought them all into the dining room so I could tape my own family to the chairs around the table. My mother's wrists are all that's left. She doesn't struggle, just puts her arms behind her, crossing her wrists. Because it's me, she makes it easy.

"Make sure they're tight!" Kidar Frenzid yells.

I do. I'm six. I only know to do as I'm told. Besides, I'm afraid.

The room is gold. The curtains are heavy saffron and thrown open. The carpet's a matching gold shag. Sunbeams light the room, refracting golden through the trees across the street. They reflect in my mother's tears as I finish her wrists. Now, my whole family sits taped to chairs, their tear-stained faces shining gold. My brother was the only one who struggled. He's eight.

My sister looks angelic. She's four.

Everything's gold.

Laughing, Kidar Frenzid pulls a gun from beneath his long, gray jacket. Later, I'll assume he had it tucked into the back of his pants.

Now, though, only sheer horror tears through my skull as, one by one, he shoots my family between their eyes. First my father, then my brother, then my mother.

The bullets are poppers. They explode inside their targets, turning their heads into caverns. Firing from a foot away, small claws pop from the bullets' sides as they fly, guarantee-

ing they won't go right through their destinations before they pop.

He leaves my baby sister for last, smiles at the horror washing over her face as she begins to comprehend what's happening. Then he gently rests the barrel against her temple. The tape across her mouth turns her pleas to muffled moans. Her blue eyes, welling with tears, stare into mine. Kidar Frenzid pulls the trigger, filling the room with an explosion, splashing me in her blood, showering me with pieces from her skull.

The room is no longer gold. It's red. Red and full of death.

I jolt upright from where I'd been sleeping with my head against the shoulder of the woman next to me on the bus to Punta Tombo. My eyes snap open. Behind my eyes, my heart thunders, slowing as I realize it was only the dream again. The dream same that has kept the experience fresh in my mind throughout the past six years, making certain I remember it as vividly as I do boarding this bus illegally this morning.

Since my escape I've learned what's hard and what's easy when you're an under-developed twelve-year-old. Acquiring money is challenging. Getting onto buses without tickets is a cakewalk—just muster up tears, call for Momma, and climb aboard.

The rocket-shuttle probably won't be so easy. I haven't seen the man following me yet today. My guess is he assumed I'd jump the ML. Odds are, he's already in Punta Tombo, waiting for me.

Outside, dried dirt hills cracked with clutches of sage streak by in the dim light of morning as we hover smoothly eastward. I sit back and close my eyes again, wondering what to do about the man in the hat.

After all, I *am* a weapon.

I fall restlessly back to sleep.

The bus decompressing awakens me as it drops loudly to rest at the stop on the coast.

The air feels hotter here when I step out with my pack. It's more humid, and tastes of salt. The Atlantic is close—I hear gulls—but see nothing but dust roads and old buildings. No sign of my faithful follower yet, either.

A dark-skinned boy sells papers from a cart, holding one over his head, calling to passersby. Old-tech papers, nearly a half-inch thick, barely flexible. Not like the ones in Americanada. The front page is devoted to the UTSC Treaty, of course. Nothing else has been in the news for months.

In two days, Mindy Reno, Earth's representative for Extraterrestrial Technology Affairs will be signing an agreement with the United Technological Species Coalition. It will happen at the Freedom Center on a planet called Orbano in the Caliban system. Everyone in the Coalition adheres to the same rules and shares technology with each other. It's not an easy group to join. Certain milestones must have been reached by societies before applications are even considered. Among others, such criteria involves scientific, philosophic, and religious concerns. A close examination of a species' history is also taken into account.

Judging from what I've read, Earth and humanity barely made the cut.

But we did, and in forty-eight hours it'll be official. Humankind will have access to technology and information they otherwise wouldn't reach for centuries.

Jumping the evolutionary ladder like this is exciting for most people, but not all. Some believe entering into the UTSC Treaty is a huge mistake. Mostly these are people currently in power, because—at the basic level— technology and information *are* power. When they shift, so will the economic balance of the planet.

Six months ago, a week before my escape, Kidar Frenzid took Providence, my twin sister, away from the Compound. I believe he set out for Orbano to use her as a weapon of negotiation to make sure the Treaty stays unsigned.

Whether his plans prove successful is not my concern. Getting Providence back alive, is. She's in the custody of a madman who I know firsthand is capable of unspeakable atrocities.

I must save her.

Pictures of my parents, brother and sister, taped to chairs, blood splattered across gold—grotesque images flash in my mind, accompanied by spiking pain. I can't think of them so close together. I force myself not to, and the hurt subsides.

I ask the newsboy for directions. He points up the hill. "Follow to the main road then left, along the seaside five miles." Gesturing to the yellow cars hovering idly outside, he asks, "Need a cab?"

"No."

Walking gives you a tactical advantage, especially in locations unknown to both you and the enemy. You *see* more.

Oh there I go. Thinking like a weapon, again.

At the top of the street, I'm greeted by the ocean. Gulls wheel against a robin's egg sky interrupted by the occasional tuft of white. I've swum in the ocean twice since my escape. Both times I felt closer to understanding God.

When you've spent you're life underground, you don't realize how breathtakingly beautiful the planet's surface is.

Soon, I see the security fences of the ISS Launch Station in the distance. Behind them, the rocket-shuttle waits on its launch track, pointing majestically skyward, maybe twenty degrees from vertical. Sunlight glints off its edges.

The Free Space Embassy, directly across from the ML station, is the only way into the complex. The MagLev's been and gone. By now, my friend with the hat knows I wasn't on it.

I leave the street, approaching the embassy toward the east side where two doors, surrounded by shrub and trees, allow access. They aren't as public as the main door, but the man following me knows my patterns. It's time to break them.

But he's a step ahead of me. Two meters from the doors, he appears from behind a tangle of brush with a gun in his hand. It's small—but that hasn't meant anything in a long time.

"It's over Nash," he says. A high-frequency tone pulls my attention to the subvocal-set clipped to his ear, its transmitter narrower than human hair. "Target apprehended," he subvocalizes. Whoever's on the other end relays rendezvous point coordinates. A team's assembled fifteen minutes away to take me back.

I cock an eyebrow. "Fifteen minutes away? Awfully chancy, isn't it? This close to the embassy?"

His eyes widen. I shouldn't be able to hear subvocs. Normal people can't and, judging by his reaction, he thinks I'm included in that group. But I can hear and manipulate nearly any frequency. "See?" I say. "When you work for top secret organizations? They always neglect to tell you the *little* things. You know, stuff that might save your life. Like what I'm capable of."

He waves the gun. "Let's go."

I stand there, pack over my shoulder, and slowly close my fingers into fists. A ringing builds from his subvocal-set, soon so loud I'm surprised *everyone* can't hear it. His eyes roll like he's been slugged in the back of his head. Unfortunately, it doesn't knock him out. He rips the unit from his ear, dropping it to the grass.

The gun comes up. It's shaky. So's his voice. "Whatever you just did doesn't matter. I know where to go. Now move!"

I stay calm. "You can't kill me. I'm too valuable. And they're waiting for you."

A rivulet of sweat runs from beneath his hat.

I sigh. "Look, I really don't want to hurt you. Just leave. Please?"

He laughs—nervously. "You're a kid. I've got the gun. Quit playing games."

I look at the security fence as the thirty minute launch warning buzzes. "Listen. I'm running out of time. You're leaving me no choice—"

He lunges at me. I dodge, close my eyes, and bring my fists to my chest.

Unsurprisingly, his gun's loaded with poppers—the same bullets Kidar Frenzid shot my family with—inhumane bullets, made to do the most severe damage possible. This time, though, they explode inside their clip, blowing the man's arm and a small chunk of his head completely away. I quickly reach inside his jacket, pulling out his spare clip as he crumples and falls to the ground. Emptying the poppers from the clip into my pocket, I spot the subvocal-set in the grass. That goes into another pocket.

I rush inside just as the explosions bring a stream of people outside. A woman shrieks. Two security men march past me in the hall, their boots clicking on the marble floor. The sign over the door they leave unguarded reads VIP AND DIPLOMATS.

I take it, and, just like that, I'm inside the complex. A coil wraps inside my stomach as I pause to catch my breath, pushing away mental pictures of Kidar Frenzid shooting my family, leaving headless bodies taped to kitchen chairs.

Shuddering, I nearly vomit.

I hate hurting people.

Rocket-shuttles aren't like buses. They're expensive, which means all seats are generally accounted for. Luckily, they have lots of storage space beneath for baggage. The compartment's fully pressurized—to facilitate pets—and barely half full. Sneaking past the fat guys in charge of loading isn't even a challenge. I crawl into the back corner, tucking myself behind my bag.

I'm small on purpose and it definitely has its advantages.

Seven hours later, having sat cramped for the rumble of takeoff, the hard turbulence breaking through the atmosphere, and now the slow process of docking, I'm relieved to feel the rocket-shuttle latch with the ISS. Within ten minutes, the baggage hatch hitches open and the handlers unload. They aren't like the guys on the ground. These men are fast. I realize very quickly I won't be able to sneak past them.

My legs are incredibly stiff as I shoulder my pack and ready myself on fingertips and toes. One large bag separates me from them. When they drag it out, I scuttle right behind, pushing past them, nearly slipping as I leap down onto the metal landing with a clang.

"Hey! Kid! There's a kid in here!" There's two of them. Unfortunately, it's the tall and lean one with the strong legs who decides to chase me. The room is dark. Our shoes slam against the catwalk, echoing in long bounces. The docking room is huge. Every ten meters or so, narrow metal steps head up or down. He's gaining on me too fast for me to consider taking the stairs.

I pump harder. My legs ache. My chest burns.

I'm about to give up, turn around, and start making up some story when a voice whispers up the stairway beside me. "Nashville? That you? Nashville Beaumont?"

I always planned to turn and run as fast as possible upon meeting anyone who knew my name.

Something makes me hesitate, though. He doesn't *sound* like one of Them. My chest heaves. My mind races for a decision. The luggage handler, a step away from nabbing me, helps. I turn to the darkened stairs. "Yes?"

A tall black man steps up, his fingers on the rail. I don't know him. He wears a rusty turtleneck beneath a black jacket. Holding out his hand, he stops the luggage guy from grabbing my arm. "He's with me."

"But he . . . was *in* with the luggage."

"He's with me."

The firmness of the repeated statement sends the baggage handler away. The black man holds out his hand, long fingers, pink tips. "I'll help you down."

I stay put. "Who are you? How do you know my name?"

"My name's Lawrence," he says. "Tyrone Lawrence. I know everything about you. I also know Kidar Frenzid's on his way to Caliban with your sister."

So much for intuition. I step back. "Only people from the Compound know these things." I glance down the catwalk, wondering how much farther I can run.

"That's not true. We also know what Kidar Frenzid did to your family." He looks away, grows quiet. "We were too late to stop it. I'm sorry."

I'm panicked because I don't know what to do. Mainly because I don't understand. "Who is *we*? Who the hell are *you*?"

His warm, brown eyes settle on mine. "We're on your side, Nash. There's always two sides. We're the *good* guys."

I consider this. *Are* there always two sides? My brain sweeps my memory for precedent. He continues before I find any.

"We want to help you now. Together, let's stop Kidar Frenzid and get Providence back." He reaches out again. "Let me take you to Orbano."

Pushing my blonde hair off my face, I search his eyes, finding no hint of deception. I haven't met many honest people, but he somehow feels like one. Something about him—strangely—reminds me of my father.

My father, taped to that chair, begins forming in my mind. Quickly, I shift gears and take the man's hand.

Tomorrow morning, Tyrone Lawrence's ship will fly us to the Caliban system. He gets me my own room on the ISS and, before retiring to bed, takes me to dinner at the Starlight Lounge.

A six-story restaurant with transparent walls, the Starlight Lounge is funnel shaped; each level smaller than the one above. It hangs like a plumb bob from the bottom center of the station, slowly rotating, offering an ever-changing view of the Earth, moon, and stars.

We sit at one of the four tables on the lowest floor. The others are empty. I order the same meal as Lawrence: a Texas porterhouse. Outside, the Earth spins into view—western Europe's covered in clouds, but the African coast glitters like a string of freshwater pearls. It would be beautiful if I didn't feel so unsettled. "Who did you say you worked for again, Mr. Lawrence?"

"Tyrone." He sips his wine. He's calm, his voice deep and soothing. "And I didn't. I said we were the good guys. Hopefully that's enough. You must know how these top secret things work." He wipes his lips, returning the napkin to his lap.

Slowly I shake my head, considering. "I don't think it will be enough,. I've come too far. I can't . . . I hope you . . . " I don't know how to finish.

Turns out I don't have to. "I understand. I'll just have to trust you the way you're trusting me." He lifts his glass. "I work directly for the President of the United States."

My pulse kicks into a gallop. "The president has no idea about the Compound," I say, my suspicion obvious.

He raises his palm. "Now calm down, Nash, and think a minute. *They* told you that. And, actually, they didn't lie. They have no idea. Truth is, they've been on our radar from the start. We've had men inside ever since the UTSC talks began." Another sip of wine. He laughs. "We never planned on finding you, though. No, you were just a happy accident."

The view outside crosses over the Middle East. There are no accidents, in my experience. Especially happy ones.

The waitress—an actual *person*—sets our dishes on the table. The smell is almost enough to relieve my worries.

"Want some advice?" Tyrone asks, lifting a fork. "Enjoy your meal. This place is a once in a lifetime experience and it's on the president's tab. Tomorrow morning you'll meet the rest of my crew and I think you'll feel much better about things."

Blood pools on my plate as I cut into my perfectly grilled steak.

That night, I have the dream again, maybe worse than ever. It wakes me early. I don't want to chance going back to sleep, so I order breakfast and watch stars in my cabin window until Tyrone comes for me.

His ship, the *Iron Heart*, is stunning. I know from my training she's a Mosquito-Class vessel with a FoldSpace drive but this one's designated FS-V. Far as I knew, the latest models were only FS-III. This lessens my worries, reinforcing his claim of working for the president.

As I'm introduced to the crew, I don't get that same warm feeling.

Tyrone's pilot, Haley Frost, looks like she stepped out of a MatrixRaveRoom. She has chopped and spiked midnight blue hair, wrapped with a thick red band, and genetically enlarged lips, also blue. Her bangles clang when I shake her hand. She smells like a garden, and has dark eyes. I don't like the smell or her eyes, but I could be too young to fully appreciate them.

I feel better about Catherine Walker. Tall and solid, she has dark brown hair and light brown skin. She looks directly into my eyes as we shake hands. "She's our security officer," Tyrone informs me.

It confuses me. "security officer? There's only four of you. Why do you need a security officer?"

I look to her to answer, but she looks to Tyrone. He smiles. "Government policy," he says. I suppose it makes sense.

The last crewmember gives me the willies.

He's simply called Lug, and is easily seven feet tall. A one-inch ring pierces his septum. His arm muscles bulge like cypress trunks from his sleeveless shirt. He's bald other than a thick black braid hanging to his waist. His arms, neck, and head are covered in tribal tattoos. Apparently he's the ship's engineer. He resembles none of the engineers from the Compound, but I suppose that's good.

A quick ship tour follows. It's a small vessel. The bridge, a hexagonal room with a forward window and two workstations, makes up most of it. Currently, blast shields cover the window. A hatch in the floor between the stations drops down to the single-person cockpit.

Six cabins split over two levels are squeezed along one side of the bridge. The mess, tactical room, and head run along the other. A final corridor leads out back, tunneling between the dual FoldSpace drives.

Tyrone informs me engineering is accessed through a hatch in the floor. On the FS-III models, I remember that hatch leading to the recreation room, and the drives being accessed through ceiling panels. He doesn't open the bomb-blast door sealing the floor panel, but I'm not surprised. Ships built for the president probably include custom modifications. Still, I'm bothered a bit when I see the ceiling panels still recessed in the hall, but I don't mention anything.

Returning to the bridge, Tyrone sits at one of the workstations. "Haley! Course plotted?"

"Aye, Cap'n," she says sliding down into the cockpit, barely touching the steps. "Locked and loaded. Time to Caliban approximately three hours, fifteen minutes." A pause and then: "ISS reports us go for departure."

"Take us out."

I wait for the shield blocking the forward window to open, but it still hasn't, even after I feel us break away from the station.

"I'll be in my quarters," Catherine Walker says.

Tyrone throws me a wink. "You should probably do the same."

I spend the time reviewing information about Caliban on my Digimate™.

.CLICK.

Caliban's actually a binary star system with two completely independent planetary groupings in stable orbit with each other. Three of the planets orbiting Caliban and one orbiting Moth—the secondary star—are categorized as terrestrial, with Earth-type atmospheres. It's considered the economic heart of our region of the galaxy.

Orbano, the capital planet, has only sixty-five percent of Earth's mass. Three different races occupy three of its five continents (two of the continents are uninhabitable polar regions). The races are so distinct, they rarely interact. The Angamon run the United

Technological Species Coalition. The other two aren't even members. One, called Skelt, are savage plant creatures still in an Iron Age. The second, the Phohonese, are short, respectful people who long ago rejected technology for a religion bearing some similarities to Earth's Hinduism, Buddhism, Taoism, and Sophism.

On the holo, Angamons kind of resemble the aliens reported by UFO abductees in the twentieth century—the ones that came to be referred to as Greys. But their description—tall and white, partially translucent with oval eyes—make them sound more like ghosts. I guess I'll find out when we arrive.

.CLICK.

Maybe that's what has me so anxious, meeting the Angamons. Or maybe it's Tyrone. Or maybe it's the prospect of finding my sister. Or maybe it's the thought of coming face-to-face once again with Kidar Frenzid.

There's just too many possible reasons.

.CLICK.

Strangely, with all their emphasis on technology, the Angamon rely almost exclusively on organic construction. They almost act as gardeners. Structures are planted, tended to, and grown.

Most governmental offices in the lake district in Ghat—including the Peace Center where the treaty signing takes place—resemble spores or mushrooms sprouting from the water or land. Some cluster together, others connect through suspension bridges made from high-tensile fiber-carbon nanonets. The organics contain phosphorus, and the nanonets are equipped with fiber-optics. At night, everything glows in royal colors of purple, emerald, ruby, and sapphire, while the lakes reflect Orbanos's two moons overhead. They shine like bright charms dangling from a bracelet of stars.

Because of all this beauty, all important business is conducted at night.

.CLICK.

Especially UTSC signings.

On final approach, I return to the bridge. The front window shields have been removed. Tyrone's still in the same chair. Lug sits at the other. It barely contains his bulk.

Orbano's space station bears no resemblance to the ISS. It looks like delicate cotton pulled thinly across the cosmos; a gossamer spider web of wispy tendrils, each one reaching out to welcome vessels.

There's something else. Something I don't notice until we draw nearer: "It's huge," I say, almost in a whisper.

Haley pops her head up from the cockpit. Some spikes of hair have fallen, and her face glistens slightly of sweat. "They want full-auto, cap."

Ignoring the look Lug throws him, Tyrone says, "Give it to 'em."

Dropping back down, Haley transfers override to Orbano Station. The *Iron Heart* quiets; the vibration and hum disappear. It's like we're attached to a kite string, riding a gentle breeze as we're reeled into the bay and its fabric wraps around and latches.

Standing, Tyrone stretches and looks at me. "Let's go find your sister."

We disembark to find an Orbanoan representative waiting. Even after preparing myself, I almost stop at the sight of him/her/it. The Angamon's a foot taller than even Lug, with a delicate thin body. Its arms and legs are long and slender, ending in swirls that remind me of Christmas decorations. It appears feather-light, gently blowing in a wind I can't feel. Its skin looks like gauze.

"Greetings," it says. Its accent so odd, I barely understand. "I be Mindastla, Angamon male." As it speaks, it changes, yet its basic form remains. The hollow gray eyes stretch and shrink. It's simultaneously beautiful and grotesque. "I learned your English special so would not we need a translator use."

"Perhaps a translator use we should," Haley whispers. Catherine shushes her.

Tyrone salutes. "General Tyrone Lawrence. Human male. United States. We're most appreciative of this most generous gesture."

General Lawrence? What happened to Captain? My stomach turns over.

"Understand we you anxious are to meet with your terror others."

"Yes, friend, if it's convenient."

Others? *What* others? Did he say *terror*?

"Come, follow." In a breath, Mindastla turns through himself and heads away, appearing to float. We follow with difficulty. Other than running lights pulsing along the sides of the floor, the corridor's transparent. It's beautiful, but hard to convince my brain that I'm not stepping out into nothingness as I proceed.

Four Orbanoans float past the other way. Their forms change as Mindastla's did as he spoke. They gesture with their hands like they're conversing, but they make no sound. "Do they usually communicate telepathically?" Catherine whispers. "Maybe most of them are mute."

"Wish ours was," Haley says. Catherine shushes her.

Mindastla leads us to a space elevator. We enter the transparent box running on a twisted nanonet cable between the station and the planet's equator. We fall and my breath catches, not from vertigo, but the view: a bright braid of stars fading to a watery blue as we plunge into the atmosphere.

At the bottom, I immediately notice the gravity difference. It's like I'm a little child again as I step onto the white sand. It's so hot, I feel the heat on my chin. Mindastla tells us not to worry. "Affair tonight happens north many spaces." Nobody asks how big a space is.

"Now go we." He becomes completely still for several seconds before raising his arm and pawing the air seven times. There's a shimmer and he disappears. Startled, we look among ourselves, but before anyone speaks, we begin disappearing too.

One by one.

It feels like diving under the sea—staying down deep until you can't possibly hold your breath any longer. Then you rise, watching the sky brighten, feeling the pressure diminish, Then finally breaking the surface, gasping for air.

We break the surface north many spaces, ending up on a nanonet suspension bridge somewhere in what appears to be the lake district of Ghat. I guess this from the lakes spreading out in every direction beneath us; it's a collection of emerald ponds attached by thin arteries. Sunlight skips across the water rippling under the light breeze.

Mindastla continues across the bridge, asking us to follow. I have to force my attention away from the incredible view to follow.

We enter a yellow-green mushroom structure. It's like entering a blood cell. Thin, organic material stretches tightly, forming walls, ceilings, floors—everything. It's all alive. I smell it before noticing a section of the wall actually throbs.

"Oh God, I'm gonna puke!" Haley pushes back outside, her hand over her mouth.

Tyrone waves Mindastla off when it glances back, concerned. "Don't worry," he tells it. "She's fine."

We continue following twisty corridors of tissue another thirty meters before our host stops, turning to a purple-veined violet membrane-wall. "There's been no communication?" Tyrone asks.

"You asked none." Mindastla says. His swirly hand makes a backwards S shape and the membrane dissolves, revealing a room behind it. My attention snaps to the man on the floor in the corner with the girl huddled beside him.

It's Kidar Frenzid. Anger pumps from my heart. I begin clenching my fists.

Tyrone's hand on my shoulder stops me. "There'll be time for that later."

I'm so consumed with hatred, I almost miss it. But I don't. The man in the hat didn't even know my capabilities. Yet this . . . this *general* . . . knows my tells. Before I fully consider this, I realize my rage blinded me also to the girl beside Kidar Frenzid. "Providence?" I ask.

She stares back. There's no recognition in her eyes, only fear.

"Don't be afraid," I say. "I'm your brother. I'm Nashville. We're twins. I won't hurt you." I step into the room. She pulls her legs up, cuddling closer to Kidar Frenzid.

"I don't have a brother." She glances into Kidar Frenzid's face. "Right, Daddy?" His arm around her tightens, but he doesn't answer.

Stunned, I shake my head. "Why would you think *he's* your father? Do you have any idea who he *really* is? He killed my entire family." Pain flashes in my skull. "And he made me watch."

More pain. I struggle through it, though. "My entire family."

"Then I can't be your sister if your whole family's dead."

An explosion goes off behind my eyes. My hands clasp the sides of my head. "You *are* my sister! We're twins!"

Again she looks to Kidar Frenzid. He doesn't take his eyes from me.

"He's not your father. He killed everyone I loved. My mother, father, brother . . . "

Another explosion. I hear this one and it nearly deafens me. I scream. My brain's on fire.

She screams louder. "Then I *can't* be your sister. Look at me. I'm alive!"

She's no longer in focus. My knees hit the floor. Blackness stabs at my brain. "I *know*! I *know*!" It's why I can't think of them too close together or a knife slices into my mind.

Slicing, slicing. The blackness stabs.

I fall forward. My face sinks into the moist ground.

The knife inside my head twists.

Black.

When I finally come to and the world stops spinning, I open my eyes and see . . . nothing. Blackness. Am I dead? I don't think so. My fingers touch the ground. Solid, not alien. I reach out slowly and discover I'm in a cage.

Memories burn inside me. My sister clinging to Kidar Frenzid, calling him Daddy. I can't make sense of it. When I try, the logic disparity begins stabbing my brain again, and I have to stop.

I can't think about it until it makes sense because of the pain it brings. And it won't make sense until I can think about it.

Which makes it unsolvable.

I pound the floor and, for the first time in six years, I let tears come to my eyes. They feel good. I cry harder. The darkness swallows my sobs.

Then a small voice makes me jump. "Don't. Please? Don't cry."

Sitting up, I wipe my face. "Who's there?"

"Providence. Daddy's here too. They put us in cages."

My mind scrambles. "I'm in one too. Do you know where we are?"

"In their ship, beneath the FoldSpace drives," says a voice with a slight Eastern European accent I haven't heard in six years. "They had the cages already setup, waiting in the recreation facility."

Heat rises through my skin. "I hate you!" I scream. "Why did you kill my family?" Another stab flashes white in my head.

"I didn't kill *anyone*, Nash," says Kidar Frenzid.

The anger now fully returns. "Liar! I saw. You made *sure* I watched." My brain tears. I holler in agony. "You made my sister—" I struggle to finish, but end in a scream.

"I know what's making you hurt," he says. "There's two memories fighting inside your mind that contradict each other. But you know which one's true. If you didn't, you wouldn't be here."

"I . . . I don't understand." I don't want to trust him, but the pain . . . the pain . . .

"You came for your sister, and here she is. This other thing—me killing your family—it must be a genetic memory imprint. Only, I don't know why they didn't mask your old memories."

I breathe deep. Did I leave before they finished? "I escaped. A week after you abducted her."

"He didn't abduct me."

"Let me, honey," Kidar Frenzid says. "I brought Providence here to share her technology with the Coalition."

"Daddy saved me! He's trying to save everyone!"

I struggle to grasp the truth in this. "Why do you keep calling him Daddy?"

"Because, as much as possible, she's my daughter." He pauses. "And you're my son."

I grit my teeth. "All you do is *lie!*"

"No. I developed both of you for the Compound. Cloned you from parts of my own genes combined with enhancements. I was naïve. They told me you were the first steps toward a new world peace. I never even considered military potential. When you were ready, I planned on giving you to the world."

"What about my parents?"

"You have no parents. They invented them."

Another pulse beats through my head. "Why would they do that?"

"The UTSC Treaty will return the Earth's power to its people, taking it away from the handful who have it now. They built the Compound to stop the Coalition movement. They failed. So they switched plans, deciding to lie in wait with their secret weapons—you and your sister—the only technology exclusive to them, making everyone else on earth inferior. You two are their edge. In their minds, as long as they control you, they can't lose."

"I don't understand. Lose what?"

"The war," he says.

"What war?"

"The war humans always expect, Nashville. The war humans even count on sometimes. That's why I had to bring Providence here, to share her with the Coalition, cutting those back on Earth off at the knees before they could construct a battlefield."

I desperately try to keep the pain out of my voice. "Why would they mess with my head?"

"My guess is they decided to turn you into my assassin just in case they failed to find us. Their types are always big on irony. Turned out they didn't need you, though. We took months to get here. When we did, the Orbanoans had already been warned we'd be coming with weapons that worked through communication. They gave us no chance to explain why we were here before locking us away."

"A communication weapon? That's crazy. The Orbanoans wouldn't believe that."

"Sure they would," Kidar says. "They've seen all sorts of technology, and the warning's coming from the people being welcomed into their Coalition—people the rest of our planet trusted enough to give power to."

"Why didn't you escape using Providence's powers? After all, she *is* dangerous. Just not the way they *think* she is."

A pause. "Because I oppose the use of violence, Nash. I loathe the very thought of it. Besides, it would be undermining everything I—*we*—have struggled for."

"*You* hate violence?" I ask. "Then why'd you make us into weapons?"

"That's *them* talking. *I* made you powerful. Power it-self is undefined until it's used. I honestly thought you would lead the next generation *out* of violence."

I considered this. "I . . . I hate hurting people, too."

"We all do," Providence says. "Daddy, you, and me. We *inherited* that from Daddy. He made *sure*."

Kidar breathes deep. "But I failed. Now you two could become the conduit for Earth's most violent war ever. And once again, they'll revel in their irony."

My mind shoots back through my studies on Mosquito-Class starships, trying to form a plan. Problem is, even if we escaped the cages—which I'm sure are re-inforced to Compound specifications—we'd never get through the bomb-blast door blocking the roof-hatch. We'd just be stuck in a bigger cage.

"Wait," I say, "does Providence have any powers that I don't? Something that might help us escape?"

Kidar sighs. "There's nothing we can do."

I reach into my pocket. "Oh, there might be."

At one frequency or another, everything vibrates.

I clip the subvocal-set I took from the man with the hat onto my cage. Kidar and I calculate the carbon-fibre nanotubes transverse and torsional frequencies will be high, but not higher than the unit's capabilities. I give Providence the lower of the two. Because she and I will hear nothing but the subvocal-set squealing, Kidar will listen for the cage's quiet ringing.

Providence goes first. The tone howls upwards faster and louder than I ever could make it do. In se-conds, Kidar stops her. "There!"

She sustains the vibration while I squeeze my fingers into my palms, sounding out a second tone. It's quieter than hers, the frequency rising much slower. I realize now that's why Kidar brought *her*—she *is* better than me.

My tone creeps past hers, higher and higher, until . . .

Crack!

The cage splits open. Sweat trickles down my face. My heart's in my throat.

Providence isn't even out of breath. "Now mine!" she yells.

We do hers. Then Kidar's.

"Now what?" he asks.

"My plan's got another step." I pull the poppers from my pocket. Neither of them know what they are, so I explain.

Kidar won't even touch them. "An invention with the sole purpose of inflicting pain and suffering. Why would anyone . . . ? Sometimes I'm so disgusted with my own species." He nearly breaks down. "I'll never understand humanity."

I grapple for their hands in the dark. "Help me with the cages." We pile them into a ladder. I climb up to place the poppers around the hatch, only: "There's nothing to hold them."

"I will," Providence says.

"Weren't you listening? You'll blow your arm off."

"From down here, silly."

I pause. "You can do that?"

"You can't?"

A minute later, a dozen poppers magically levitate around the perimeter of the bomb-blast cover, while we crouch in the room's back corner. "You sure you got em?" I ask. I can't see anything, but I imagine she's struggling.

"Yep, no problem. Can I help explode 'em, too?"

She's better than me. I can't believe it. "Sure."

Kidar counts to three. I bring my fists to my chest. Who knows what Providence does, but the poppers blow like a concussion bomb, popping the bomb-blast cover straight up. It bounces off the ceiling and thuds onto the main floor.

"Holy," Providence says.

"Yeah." I climb to the main deck and dash to my room, pulling my Digimate™ from my pack as they come up. "We've got ten, maybe fifteen minutes." Sitting on my bed, I flip through menus.

Providence holds Kidar's hand. "Why aren't we leaving?" she asks.

"My plan's got another step." I smile.

We enter the Peace Center just as Mindy Reno finishes signing the Treaty, sealing Earth's entry into the Coalition.

Managing to make our way from the *Iron Heart* to the space elevator and down to the surface hadn't been hard. Using the teleport-transit system was trickier. We ended up falling back on our "terrorist" status, threatening some poor Orbano civilian into helping.

Reno waves the Treaty above her head. "It's a big day for Humanity!" she announces. A quiet cheer follows. Mostly Orbanoans are present, and they don't cheer. Not like us, anyway.

The Orbanoan President of the UTSC standing on the podium beside Reno suddenly cocks her head sideways. She's been alerted to something. The same thing happens to other Orbanoans stationed around the room. The crowd noise dissolves to puzzled murmurs as her head continues jerking. She seems distressed. Reno asks if she's okay. Of course, she can't answer.

Across the room, Tyrone stands with his crew. He glances around, his eyes narrowed, concerned.

Then he spots us, standing by the entrance.

"Hey! They're terrorists!" he yells, running our way. "Get them!" Orbanoans follow, gliding swiftly, yet still graceful.

We don't move.

Two Orbanoans reach us the same time as Tyrone. "That's them," he says. "The terrorists."

But they're not interested in us. They want him and his crew who, as of one minute ago, are in full breach of their species' treaty with the Coalition.

"Wait!" Tyrone yells as thick orange vines sprout from the floor, wrapping quickly around his legs and arms before hardening. The same thing happens to his crew. Even Lug can't struggle free as the Orbanoans simply tip them over, and carry them out like fallen logs.

They'll be put on trial, and an enforcement team will launch for Earth to deal with the rest of the Compound. Likely, everyone involved will be sentenced to death.

It has to be this way, I suppose. We're no longer playing against ourselves. We're in a league. Rules must be enforced.

Still, I really *do* hate violence.

Mindy Reno approaches. "What just happened?"

We start explaining, but we can't. There's simply too much.

It's she who finally gives up. "Just tell me again. You're *sure* there's no presidential involvement?"

"Yes. At least as sure as I can be."

"Well, thank God for small mercies. One thing—what changed their minds about you being terrorists?"

I tell her about the Orbanoans passing by in the station corridor, gesturing as though conversing, but making no sound.

She nods. "They don't communicate vocally."

"No, they do. Just not at a frequency *regular* humans can hear. I can, though. They speak in voices just beneath microwave range. So loud, in fact, I hear them everywhere, especially up on the station. Before we left the *Iron Heart* to come here, I programmed my Digimate™ to analyze frequencies in that range, breaking out lexicon patterns while we made our way to the space elevator. By the time we were on the ground, it was able to splice together a rough message in their language."

I nod to Providence. She holds up my Digimate™ connected to the subvocal-set. "And she broadcast that message to the room."

Mindy Reno's obviously impressed. "And what did the message say?"

"The truth. We told them who we really are. And I knew the Orbanoans would give credence to it because they put extremely high regard in anyone taking the effort to learn their language and culture. Their society is built on respect."

She scratches her head. "Wow. And here I thought they were mute," she says, tucking a fallen lock of auburn hair behind her ear. "Well, except that one who kinda speaks English."

.CLICK.

I carefully consider my words before speaking. Doesn't matter, silence compresses into one parameter: empty-time. Silence costs nothing.

Sometimes.

"My name's Nashville Beaumont. My sister's Providence Beaumont. Our father is Kidar Frenzid. Few people know we exist. Even fewer know our role in Earth's signing of the UTSC Treaty.

"This Digimate™ contains a historical record of everything I've experienced since my—" I stumble on the word only slightly this time "—*birth* twelve years ago. It also holds detailed information of an underground military facility so secret even the President of the United States of Americanada won't know about it until the Orbanoans coming to Earth provide him and every other world leader a copy of this recording. I implore all of you to disseminate this information to every human citizen. Not for the sake of awareness—but as a *warning.*"

"What happened in Texas *cannot* ever happen again.

A handful of people *cannot* control an entire planet while everyone else sits idly by. In some ways, you're as much to blame as they are—nobody has control unless they're given it.

"And people don't *have* to be hurt. There's been enough war. That's why—for now—I'm staying here on Orbano with my sister and father."

.CLICK.

I reconsider my ending.

.CLICK.

"My name's Nashville Beaumont. My sister's Providence Beaumont . . ."

" . . . and we're the reason you're now free."

I found myself stranded in the Ukraine one very cold winter, and was looking for an idea for a story I could finish in one sitting to keep my fingers moving so I wouldn't freeze to death. I got the idea to riff off an Elvis song. This was one of the few times I had absolutely no clue what my ending was going to be before I started writing. I did know the cat would somehow be involved though . . .

The King is Dead

The gun barrel presses against Virginia's cheek. It's cold, but then most things are these days. She's always cold. Must be something about hitting sixty-five, because it seemed to start around eight months ago, on her birthday.

Her eyes glance to the left. Although the weapon set against the side of her head looks similar, Virginia decides that it's definitely not a Beretta nine-millimeter—the only gun, other than this one, to ever touch her skin.

"All right lady, you got till three. Then I pull the trigger."

Jimmy is the name of the man doing the counting, not that they've been introduced or anything. He is a large man—probably close to six feet tall and over two hundred and eighty pounds, Virginia guesses. He smells like Marlboros and cloves, the way she remembers her late husband Stephen smelling a couple of years before his death, back when he still smoked. Even though the temperature in the room is seventy-two degrees, sweat runs down the sides of Jimmy's face.

"Have you been tested for diabetes?" Virginia asks.

"What the fuck business is that of yours?" Jimmy asks.

"You should look after yourself. While you're still young."

"Yeah? And you should shut the fuck up while you're still alive." Then, turning to the other man in Virginia's living room, he says, "Can you believe this old broad?"

When the two of them broke in fifteen minutes ago, Virginia instantly felt attracted to Jimmy—large, strong men with a sense of control have always been her weakness. The second man—luckily the one without a gun—is a different story. He is the only part of this equation that makes her nervous.

"All right," Jimmy says, "I'm countin'. You got three." He repositions the gun against Virginia's temple.

He's waiting for her to tell him where she keeps the "valuables". An expression that sounded so much like he pulled it out of a movie that it took everything Virginia had not to smile when he said it. But she knows he's heard she has *something*, but judging by his vagueness, even *he* probably isn't quite sure what that something is. Could be either of two things. Of the two, Virginia hopes it turns out to be the car, because the other thing would most certainly be a mistake.

A rather *big* mistake.

"One," Jimmy says.

"Yeah! One for the money!" yells the other man. He needs a shave. His hair is black, greasy, and thin, and his voice is fast and high-pitched. *Like a Carney*, Virginia thinks. *Never trust a Carney.* "Sorry, I got caught up in the excitement," he says.

Jimmy cocks the slide on the gun. "Two."

"For the show!" Yells man number two, plopping himself down into Virginia's love seat and setting his boots onto her coffee table. Beside him, Lisa Marie wakes up. With her round Persian face and bright golden eyes, Virginia always thought Lisa Marie looked more like an owl than a cat. After giving the man a quick once over, Lisa Marie tucks her head back into her tail and once again becomes a big gray ball of sleeping fur. For some reason, Virginia finds solace in Lisa Marie's lack of concern.

"Three to get ready," the second man mumbles, looking around the room the same way Stephen used to do when he couldn't find the television remote. After Stephen died, Virginia got rid of the television—or The Idiot Box, as Stephen used to call it—and replaced it with the cinnamon recliner she is sitting in now.

"Get your fuckin' boots off the table!" Jimmy yells. "They are filthy."

Grudgingly the man does as he's told. "Fuck it, Jimmy. You'd think we were visitin' your ma."

"Just show a little respect," Jimmy says.

"Thank you, Jimmy." Virginia says.

"Listen lady, I like you. Don't make me blow your brains all over this chair. Tell me where I'll find the—"

"Lady, this is one fat fuckin' cat you have," the man on the love seat says, and reaches over to pat Lisa Marie. Virginia figures it's probably a mistake.

With a blur and a howl, Lisa Marie makes it known that she doesn't want to be touched. The man leaps to his feet. His right forearm is scratched deeply. It begins to well with blood. "Jesus! Freakin' cat! Go! Cat, I'm telling you, Go!" He points out of the room but Lisa Marie rolls back up on the loveseat and closes her eyes.

"Now, why should the cat go?" Jimmy asks, slowly and methodically. "You're the one sitting around like a dumb shit. The cat probably thinks *you* should go."

Dumb Shit doesn't respond. Just crosses his arms in a huff. Virginia likes Jimmy. She bets he's good to his mother.

"What's that smell?" Jimmy asks.

"Oh damn," Virginia says, "I have a saucepan on the stove." She rises from her chair but Jimmy stops her.

"You stay put. I'll take care of it."

Stuffing the gun into the back of his pants, Jimmy walks into the kitchen. Virginia watches him, admiring his solid body. She guesses him to be in his midtwenties.

"Whatcha making anyway?" Jimmy asks, lifting the lid from the saucepan before Virginia can warn him not to. Instantly, the pot erupts into flame. The pot is full of oil she was heating to deep fry her *ollie ballen* in. On the counter beside the stove, raisin speckled balls of dough are waiting to be dropped inside. Now they will have to wait a while longer.

Jimmy grabs the flaming pot's handle and runs to the sink, yelping about his fingers being burned the entire way. Virginia tries to tell him to simply put the lid back on, but he doesn't hear her over the commotion. He spins the taps beside the faucet, pouring water into the flames, causing the oil to rise. The flames lick the bottom of her kitchen curtains and they instantly are engulfed in blaze. "Christ!"

From the living room, Dumb Shit laughs as Jimmy pulls the curtain rod from the window, burning his fingers as it falls to the hardwood floor. He stomps out the fire with his boots—not quick enough to stop the smoke alarm from going off.

Minutes later, Jimmy returns to Virgnia's side, the gun back in his hand, only not the hand it was in before. That one's a bit too blistered.

"Sorry 'bout your curtains," he says. "And the smoke alarm."

"You probably clogged my sink," she says. "Never pour oil down a sink drain."

"I'll try to remember that." A thin black smoke rolls across the ceiling, filling the living room with the smell of charred drapes. Virginia frowns.

Dumb Shit picks up the terra cotta urn from the mantel. "Hey now, this looks like it might be worth something."

Before Virginia can say a word, it slips out of his hands and hits the marble floor at his feet. Ashes billow from the urn as it breaks.

"Don't you ever dust, lady?" Dumb Shit asks.

"That's actually my late husband, Stephen." She pauses and decides to clarify, just in case. "He's dead."

"Hey Numb Nuts," Jimmy says, "get a frigging grip on yourself. You just spilled her husband on the floor."

"Sorry." Picking up the large pieces of the urn, Numb Nuts steps in the ashes.

"Now you're gonna tread him all through the carpet!" Jimmy says.

"Just leave it," Virginia says.

"Just fucking *leave* it," Jimmy says and then apologizes to Virginia.

Virginia takes the opportunity to tiptoe across the metaphorical broken ice and literal chunks of busted urn. "So Jimmy, I bet your mom named you James, didn't she? We had a son named James once." Her gaze falls to the picture of James on the coffee table just left of where Numb Nuts's feet had been a few minutes before. In the picture James is in his full military dress. *Bravo Alpha One Niner*. "We lost him to Iraq."

For a minute, she senses Jimmy's sympathy. But he's quick to catch it. "Listen, lady. I don't give two shits about your kid." He pauses for a breath and picks up the picture from its place on her cherry Queen Anne coffee table. "Okay, that was out of line. I'm sorry about your son. He looks like a good kid." He shakes his head. "Goddamn fucking towel heads. Goddamn fucking Iraq."

Virginia looks up into Jimmy's eyes. "Thank you Jimmy."

Numb Nuts disappears down the hall and Virginia hears him open the door to the garage. Jimmy sets the picture of James back on the table. He seems to notice the wall full of pictures behind Virginia's chair for the first time. There are eleven of them—all framed, all different sizes. The largest one hangs directly over the fireplace. It's Virginia's favorite. Stephen's favorite had always been the one hanging right above her chair—a shot of the gates of Graceland he took himself the summer they drove down to Tennessee.

"Wow," Jimmy says, taking them all in. "You really got something for Elvis, hey?"

"Well—" she starts, but Numb Nuts cuts her off, running back into the living room.

"Boss, you ain't gonna believe what's out in the garage. A *Bonneville*. But not just any Bonneville. This one's like full cherry. I mean it's mint."

Bingo, Virginia thinks.

"Bingo!" Jimmy says. "You got the keys for that baby handy?" he asks Virginia.

Virginia nods. "They're above the sun visor on the driver's side. But it's not a Bonneville. It's a Stutz Blackhawk." She doesn't bother pointing out that it's worth probably ten times the price of a Bonneville.

"Sure looks like a Bonneville to me," Numb Nuts says. Virginia ignores him. If they don't know the value of cars, they're in the wrong business.

"Make sure she stays put," Jimmy says, and disappears down the hall, taking the gun with him. Virginia settles back into her chair, feeling the warmth of the afghan she has draped over the back pressing softly against her neck.

Numb Nuts is studying the big picture hanging above the fireplace—her favorite. "Wow! I knew the king was big when he kicked the bucket, but I never realized he was *this* big!" He studies the picture a little more. "Come to think of it, I don't remember his Goth period, either. Wait a minute! That's not the king. What's going on?" He looks at the rest of the pictures. "None of these are actually Elvis."

"No," Virginia says, "they're all my late husband, Stephen."

"Yeah? He some kind of nut job? What's with the Elvis getup? And what's with the big chunk of vampire jewelry around his neck?"

"Stephen was an Elvis impersonator. And that thing around his neck is called an 'ankh'. It's an Egyptian symbol of rebirth and fertility." In the picture, a spot light glances off the edge of Stephen's oversized talisman, making it sparkle like a fallen star. Oh how she misses him.

Numb Nuts makes a face. "Yeah? So what's he impersonatin'? I don't remember Elvis's Egyptian phase, either." He wipes his nose with his hand and then rubs it on his shirt. "I remember skinny heart-throbby Elvis, and I remember fat, pill-poppin' Elvis. But not King Tut Elvis. Then again, I don't remember Elvis ever bein' nowhere near *this* fat." He checks some of the other photos. In every one, Stephen has his oversized ankh strung around his neck. "So, really, what's with the big funny cross? You're husband—was he some kind of comedian?"

"Stephen? No, no, nothing like that. He was an Elvis impersonator, like I said. But he was also a psychic medium."

Numb Nuts laughs. "Looks like an extra, extra, large to me," he says. "Ain't nothing medium about that!"

Jimmy returns to the room. "You even know what a medium *is* Cock Jaws?"

Cock Jaws just stares back, stupidly. His mouth opens, but no infinite wisdom cometh.

"It means he could speak with spirits and shit," Jimmy says. "You know, talk to the dead. That kind of stuff."

Cock Jaws peers at the picture. "Yeah? No shit." He flashes a look to Virginia. "This for real? Like that kid in that movie? The one who saw dead people?"

Virginia just shrugs. "Never saw it."

"How did he go?" Jimmy asks.

Virginia looks away. "He had an . . . accident on stage."

"What kind of accident?" Jimmy asks. "You mean while he was doing Elvis?"

She nods. "One of the karate moves." She looks away, across the room. It's not something she likes re-membering. "Usually he only got down so far." She leans forward and holds her palm about a foot and a half from the floor, still looking away from the men. "This time the stage had been recently waxed and he ended up going all the way. He did the full splits. Hyper-extended his groin." She ended it there. They didn't need to know any more than that. Nobody did.

And certainly nobody needs to know too much about the rest. About that week of hell. About the gun. About the ceremony.

Jimmy winces. "Serious? He tore out his crotch and died?" Jimmy asks. "Them's some tough breaks."

Closing her eyes, Virginia just nods. *That's close enough.*

"That's fucked up," Cock Jaws says. "I'm guessing he ripped the ass pretty much right out of that eagle suit."

He guessed right. By far, it was Stephan's favorite outfit, and thinking of the sound it made it when it tore that night during the final chorus of "Hunka Hunka Burnin' Love" still made Virginia cringe. A thunderous split, loud enough to be heard above the music—half white leather, half groin muscle and tissue.

Virginia spent a good five hours attempting to sew Stephen's suit back up so his body could be buried in it. The memory comes to mind now bringing a well of despair with it. She feels that old familiar twist in her stomach. She misses that body a lot most days. In the end, she never did get any of it to look quite right again. That was one of the main reasons she had decided on cremation.

Cock Jaws laughs. "Kinda funny now, hey? I mean, he bein' dead and all. Maybe we should be tryin' to talk to *him*." With the last word, Cock Jaws hits the portrait with his finger, applying just enough pressure to click the secret latch open behind it. The picture levers forward on its hinges ever so slightly. *Oh, sugar,* Virginia thinks. *Here we go. This is where it all goes bad.*

But Cock Jaws doesn't even notice. His attention has moved on to Virginia's spoon collection hanging beside the window over the loveseat. Unfortunately, Jimmy's a little more astute. He heard the latch before the picture even moved. Virginia doubts much gets past him.

He looks at Cock Jaws. "You not even gonna wonder why that picture's on hinges, Dick Brain?" Jimmy asks him. "Or would you rather just admire those spoons?"

Dick Brain looks back to the big picture of Stephen swinging his arm during "CC Rider", his chain and ankh and white eagle suit bathed in blue spot lights . "Holy Toledo, you're right," Dick Brain says. He swings the picture fully out, revealing the safe underneath. "Well hello there, my friend. What have we here?" He gives Virginia a sideways glance. "What's the combination, lady?"

She ignores him.

"Hey, I asked you a question. What's the combination to the secret safe?" He looks to Jimmy. "Put the gun back against her head. She'll start talking."

But Jimmy isn't paying attention to Dick Brain. He's studying the photos. In particular, he's interested in the one behind Virginia—the photograph of the gates of Graceland. "I don't need to," he says. "I know the combination."

This confuses Dick Brain. "How? Did I miss somethin'?"

Jimmy walks over and pushes him out of the way. With deft fingers, he spins the dial on the safe. "Three, thirty-seven, four." He says the numbers out loud as he turns to them. When he's done, he takes a step back and rubs his hands together. "And the safe," he says, "of course, clicks open." With a gentle pull of the handle, the door swings toward him, opening wide.

"What?" Dick Brain asks. "How the fuck did you—"

Jimmy nods to the picture of Graceland. "The gates, Shit Head. Look at the address."

Shit Head looks. "Well, I'll be damned." Virginia finds this comment subtly ironic. At least she can take some entertainment value in that.

Squinting, Jimmy looks into the darkness of the safe's interior. "Whoa," he says, and reaches slowly inside.

From the corner of her eye, Virginia sees Lisa Marie look up attentively from the her place on the love seat. Virginia sighs regretfully. They should have just left with the car. "I strongly recommend you leave those be," she says, calmly. She knows she's wasting her time, though, but at least she can feel she tried.

"Yeah I bet you do," Jimmy says. He pulls a pair of shoes out of the safe. The only other thing inside it is Stephen's ankh, still on its thick silver chain.

The shoes are a deep blue and the suede sparkles brightly in the cozily lit room. As usual, the sight of them makes Virginia's breath catch in her throat slightly. The soles still glimmer with the same intensity they did when Stephen locked them away two years ago.

"Christ," Shit Head says. "Where did ya get these? Steal them off some dead pimp?"

Jimmy compares them to his own feet and smiles. "I think they're even my size." He slips his feet out of his worn brown loafers.

Virginia sees Lisa Marie come to her paws. "That's *really* not a good idea," Virginia says uselessly as Jimmy's feet go into her dead husband's blue suede shoes. "*Really* not a good idea at all, Jimmy."

But it's too late.

On the loveseat, Lisa Marie recoils into a squished sponge and then leaps up, looking very much like a stretched slinky, until she lands on Jimmy's face. His scream is muffled by her tummy as her claws dig into the back of his head and neck. She loosens one paw and, holding it out in the air, Virginia sees the claws extend much farther than they should be able to. The lamplight of the room glints off them making them appear like steely knives.

With surgeon-like precision, she thrusts the claws down and through Jimmy's chest. The white hearth of Virginia's fireplace is suddenly speckled red. Lisa Marie pulls her claws out, ripping Jimmy's heart with them in one quick splatter move. From the look of the heart and the apparent clogging through the torn arteries dangling from it, Virginia suspects the man didn't have much longer to live anyway. *What a shame.*

Lisa Marie drops the heart to the floor where it lands like a cracked egg with a broken yolk, and releases her grip from Jimmy's head, pushing herself into a backward somersault toward the loveseat. Jimmy's eyes are locked into wide surprise as he collapses onto his knees.

Shit Head is still standing there, his face frozen in shock as Lisa Marie flies toward him, this time looking more like a razor sharp torpedo than a slinky. Unlike

Jimmy, she doesn't make Shit Head's death quick and (relatively) painless.

The first slice comes horizontally across his chest, ripping the skin open the way Stephen used to cut his trout before he filleted them. Shit Head's screams are not at all muffled, and Virginia hopes she isn't disturbing the neighbors.

The claws of her one paw are still dug deeply into Shit Head's back as Lisa Marie reaches down and tears him completely open, starting at the bottom of his stomach and ending just below his throat. The two incisions together form a grotesque bloody cross for an instant until the man's organs and internals manage to push themselves through the wound with a sickly squish.

Virginia closes her eyes for moment. She is grateful a lot of the smell is masked by the burnt drapes. When she opens her eyes again, both men are in a clump on the floor and Lisa Marie is sitting beside them, licking her front paw.

Virginia has no idea how she'll ever get the blood out of her Persian carpet. Maybe vinegar and baking soda.

She stands from her chair and carefully pulls the shoes from Jimmy's feet, shaking her head. His mother would be so disappointed. No blood is on the shoes, thankfully. Virginia places them back into the safe, on top of Stephen's ankh, where they belong. She locks them back up, swinging the portrait into place once again.

From the back of Jimmy's pants, Virginia pulls out the gun and brings it into the kitchen. She opens the second drawer, the one below the cutlery, and places the gun inside, laying it with the Beretta already there. She was right, this gun is different. Similar, but different.

Closing the drawer, she goes back into the living room and sits on the loveseat. Lisa Marie jumps up into her lap.

Virginia runs her hand along the cat's back, pushing gently against her soft fur. "I tried to warn them, Stephen."

She remembers back to that day, one week from Stephen's accident, when the doctor gave them both the news: Stephen's performing days were over. He would never be able to do Elvis again. He would be lucky if he managed to ever walk without a cane. It would be years of physiotherapy and rehabilitation.

She remembers their conversation long into that night. Without Elvis, what point was there? He had no desire to go on living in a defective body. She remembers their decision. They made it together, but she went out alone the next morning and bought the Beretta and the dried bull testicles. The testicles were important.

That night, they had the ceremony, in this very room. Virginia had pushed all the furniture against the walls, and rolled up the Persian. The pentagram was outlined in sand. Unfortunately, not sand from the three sand seas — that was unattainable on short notice, forcing Virginia to improvise with a bag of sandbox sand bought from Home Center.

She laid Stephen in the center of the pentagram and she lit the candles and read from the *Zend-Avesta*. Lisa Marie watched curiously from the sidelines, not knowing the key role she played in the whole affair, as both the spirits of Osiris and Isis were called forth, along with the seven *Amesha Spentas*.

When the incantations were finished, Virginia placed the barrel of the Beretta lovingly against her husband's temple and gently pulled the trigger.

She remembers his last words. "I will never forget them, Stephen," she says, and to prove it, she recites them now. " 'Let them burn my house, Gina,' you said."

Gingerly, she rubs beneath Lisa Marie's mouth.

" 'They can steal my car — it doesn't matter. Drink my booze from a jar. Let 'em do whatever they want—' " She shakes her head slowly. " '—but just make damn sure they don't go near those shoes. Make goddamn sure nobody steps on my blue suede shoes.' "

She lets out a big sigh. Tomorrow will be a full day of house cleaning. Mr. Clean had worked that night she shot Stephan, but the blood wasn't soaked into the Persian, it was only on the hardwood floor. This would be trickier.

"Oh Stephen, I miss you sometimes," she says, and strokes the back of Lisa Marie's head.

Lisa Marie looks up into Virginia's eyes and she purrs.

The idea for this story came *from a single image I imagined: one of a young girl walking down the middle of a busy freeway, not carrying whether she lived or died. That was it. And the strange part is, that image never made it into the story. But somehow from that thought grew Deirdre, one of the most unforgettable characters I've ever come up with.*

As a side note, I entered this in the Surrey International Writers' Conference Storyteller Award competition in 2003 and, according to a secret washroom conversation with Jack Whyte, it actually made it into their top seven. But don't tell anyone. I'm not sure those sort of conversations are meant to be public knowledge.

Orchids

On her way to kill herself, Deirdre checks her reflection in the coffee shop window. *I look dead already.* She pushes her fingers into her hair and pulls her bangs down over her eyes, like a black veil. She probably looks worse, but she can't see well enough to tell now. *Perfect.*

She walks in and joins the line, wilting when she spots the girl behind the counter. Today is not a good day for the bubbly personality that likely accompanies the blonde bob and hoop earrings. With a sigh, Deirdre walks up.

"Rough night?" the girl asks.

"I spent the night in a ditch," Deirdre says without smiling. Her fingers play with her lip piercing—a nervous habit. She squints at the ridiculously overwhelming menu of choices, frustrated. "I just want a coffee."

Lobotomy girl giggles, causing the hoops in her ears to sway. "Today's features are Sumatra, Zimbabwe, Serena Organic—"

Deirdre stops her. "Look, I don't care. Whatever's strongest."

"What size?"

"Whatever's biggest."

Deirdre takes her coffee to the smoking section—a spacious area shared by fine establishments everywhere, also known as "the street". She spots an empty table as the rattling of a loud truck rumbling past catches her attention. Its cargo stares back, making her stomach convulse. Chickens, dumb and innocent, headed to the nugget machine. She shudders as it disappears from view and coffee spills over the side of her cup, burning her fingers. She turns back to the table, only to find it now occupied by a pimply guy in a faux Italian suit. *No doubt on his way to work in a mall.*

She briefly considers sitting with him but decides the woman at the table next to his will make better company.

"Mind if I sit here?" Deirdre asks.

It startles the woman. "No, not at all. Sorry, you caught me daydreaming. You know what that's like."

Deirdre shrugs off her knapsack, placing it beside her as she sits. "Not really. I side with Pascal."

The woman pulls out a Salem, taps it on the pack and puts it between her lips. She's probably ten years older than Deirdre. Thirtyish.

"Second year philosophy," Deirdre explains. "Can I bum one?"

"Pascal's okay with smoking?"

Deirdre smiles and slides a cigarette from the pack. "I'm Deirdre."

The woman reaches across and lights it, her hands smelling expensive. "You look like shit," she says. "I'm Helen."

Deirdre laughs and blows blue smoke into the morning air. "Such a charmer, Helen."

"Oh, I don't mean your style," she says, "just in general."

Deirdre scrutinizes more closely, noticing the creases around Helen's eyes, the odd liver spot, and evidence of a dye job. She decides Helen is in her late forties, which explains the comment.

The guy with the cheesy suit interrupts. "She spent the night in a ditch." He lifts his cup to Deirdre. "I was in line behind you."

Deirdre ignores him. "I actually spent the night in a bus station," she says to Helen.

"I see," Helen says, "Which one?"

"Greyhound."

"No," she smiles, "I mean where did you come from? What city?"

Deirdre points to the station across the street with the two fingers holding her cigarette. "That one. I stayed there."

Helen seems unimpressed. "I see. So where are you going?"

"The Grand Canyon."

This hits a nerve. "Oh, you'll love it! Had my first honeymoon there. Absolutely gorgeous."

"Yeah?" Deirdre says, "I'm gonna throw myself off the side." She pulls out her compact and adds more eyeliner.

Helen quickly finishes her coffee in silence and leaves.

"Nice meeting you," Deirdre says, watching in the little mirror as Helen disappears down the sidewalk. She snaps the compact closed and jumps, surprised to be staring into the eyes of Cheesy Suit Guy.

"You're so full of shit," he says.

"Why the *fuck* are you sitting at my table?" Deirdre asks, unsuccessfully trying to sound like she isn't rattled.

"You're not jumping off of anything," he says.

A bus pulls up to the curb. Shoving her compact into her knapsack, Deidre takes one last drag and stubs out her cigarette.

He smiles. "That'll kill you."

"That's my bus," she says and leaves.

"The 214?" He laughs. "Oh yeah, nonstop service to downtown Seattle and the Grand Canyon."

Deirdre sits in the only vacant seat on the bus, a side-facer near the back, surrounded by high school kids. She is squeezed between two greasy guys in denim jackets, trying to convince each other to skip first class. They look remarkably similar to Bill and Ted, and smell like

Woody Harrelson. She likes them, finding their almost illiterate discussion, consisting primarily of single syllable words, fascinating. She can't say the same about the girls sitting across from her.

Girlie girls. These very same ones attend every high school from Seattle to New York. Two years ago, they graduated with Deirdre up in Vancouver but they didn't follow her to university. After high school, girlie girls land jobs at coffee shops.

The herd always has an obvious leader, the popular girl. Invariably, she is blonde and accessorizes exclusively in pink. Deirdre hates the popular girl, but she hates the others more because they create her.

This popular girl is doodling on her subject's arms, branding them with cartoon puppies, Deirdre suspects. The way they wait so patiently for a turn under their master's pen is going to make her vomit if she keeps watching.

Bill and Ted reach an agreement and bail at the next stop. *No doubt headed to 7-Eleven.* Left to find her own distraction, Deirdre pulls a worn notebook from her knapsack. She flips through the dog-eared pages as someone plops into the seat beside her.

"By the way, I'm Pete," he says, out of breath.

It's the same guy who sat at her table outside the coffee shop. *Cheesy Suit Pete,* mall worker. She blinks at him and goes back to her book.

"Whatcha doin'?" he asks.

"Writing poetry."

He reads over her shoulder. "Cheery stuff. What do you do for fun? Burn kittens?"

She ignores him, glaring at the girls instead. They're singing.

"Why don't you write something happy?" Pete asks.

Deirdre tenses. "Because I write *good* poetry."

"It has to be depressing to be good?"

"Yes."

"Why?"

"Name one happy poem that doesn't suck ass." She rummages through her knapsack while he thinks.

"Well, I don't really read—"

She hands him a book. "Here. Good poetry."

"Sylvia Plath? Never heard of her." He opens it near the middle and reads. "She seems less depressing than you."

Deirdre snatches it back, slamming it shut. "Yeah? Well she stuck her head in an oven when she was thirty. I'd say the girl was a little depressed."

He laughs. "Stuck her head in an oven? What, she baked herself?"

"No, you tard. A gas oven?"

He laughs even louder.

"Why is that funny? What the hell is wrong with you?"

"Just seems so dramatic. Like you cannonballing into the Grand Canyon."

She returns both books to her bag. "You couldn't possibly understand. Your poetry comments made that crystal clear."

"What, exactly, does that mean? You want to kill yourself because happy poems 'suck ass'? Any idea how whacko you sound?"

Her eyes narrow. "Why are you here, anyway? Why are you even on this bus?"

"Because," he says, "you forgot to get my name and number. Can I give them to you now?"

The bus driver announces the school stop.

"No thanks," Deirdre says, intending to join the students spilling into the aisle. Unfortunately, the herd beats her to it, leaving no room. She sighs and glances up at a doodled arm, ready to gag on happy faces and true love forevers. But instead, her jaw drops.

Five lines of prose run across the brunette's shoulder, written in a stunning hand of curlicues, dipping like fish beneath the blue straps of her blouse.

"You okay?" Pete asks Deirdre.

"It's beautiful," she whispers.

"What is?"

She ignores the question. Her attention migrates to the spiky-haired blonde behind the brunette with skin also adorned by Miss Popular. The girl won't stop moving and her shirtsleeves cover most of the words. Deirdre squints, straining to read them.

Reaching up, Pete taps the girl's back. "Could you bend down? My suicidal friend wants to read your arm."

Before she can answer, the bus begins emptying and the popular girl pushes her forward. She glares back. "What am I supposed to do, Cin? Mow everybody down?"

Ladies and gentlemen, your prom queen: Cin.

Cin rolls her eyes. She smiles politely at Deirdre as the line moves ahead.

Deidre grabs Cin's arm. "Where did you read that?"

"Excuse me?"

"That poetry you put on your friends. Who wrote it?"

"You're a freak," she says, pulling free.

Deirdre grabs the purse looped over her shoulder and pulls her to a stop. "Please?"

"What? What the hell do you want?"

"Who wrote the poems?

She stares at Deirdre, confused. "Poems?"

"On their arms."

She yanks back her purse. "I did. You watched me."

"Wait!" Deirdre screams. "I mean originally."

She stops at the door. "I did."

"Really?"

"Really."

"When?"

"What are you on?"

The driver looks back angrily. "Let her leave!"

Deirdre blushes. "Just one more question? You wrote them before today, right? And just remembered them?"

Rolling her eyes, the girl exhales in exasperation and disappears through the doors.

The bus pulls from the curb. "Are you always like this?" Pete asks.

Deirdre doesn't hear. She's too busy staring out the back window, watching the school get smaller.

"Is this normal for you? Or is today some sort of exceptional day?"

"I have to get off," Deirdre whispers.

"Did you forget to take a pill, maybe?"

"I have to get off," she repeats, growing hysterical. "I have to get off!"

The bus screeches to a stop and she jumps out. She hears it leave behind her, and begins toward the school, alone.

Pete's voice forces a reassessment of the "alone" part. "So, what now?" he asks.

"What the fuck? Why are you following me?"

He shrugs. "It's one of the most interesting mornings I've ever had."

"That is just sad."

And they start walking.

They stayed together until noon, spending the morning in a park across the street from the school, underneath a redwood. Deidre sat and read Sylvia Plath in mute solitude, managing to shut out most of Pete's incessant babble. It became evident early on that he thoroughly enjoyed the sound of his voice. He only pressed her for a response once—to explain what, exactly, induced their impromptu stakeout.

"She wrote the poems this morning," Deirdre answered. "Right there, on the bus."

"Okay, but so what?"

"Are you even listening? She wrote them in *front* of us."

"I understand that. But who cares? Were they, like, super good or something?"

She nodded. "Yes. Very good."

Using a branch he found in the grass beside him, Pete scored the dirt in front of his shoes while he thought this over. A minute later, he had an epiphany. "Hey! Didn't you say all good poetry is depressing? Her stuff isn't." He paused and then asked, "Is it?"

Deirdre smiled. "No, it's not. It's beautiful."

He looked puzzled. "What about your date with the Grand Canyon?" Deirdre saw a light turn on in his brain. He understood.

They had been under the tree a couple of hours when Pete suddenly stood up and brushed the grass and dirt from his clothes.

Squinting into the sun, Deirdre asked, "What're you doing?"

"It's almost twelve, some of us do have to get to work today," he said. "These aren't just my tree sittin' clothes, you know."

"I was beginning to wonder."

"Yeah, well, those of us not leaping to our deaths this week need to make some cash." He handed her a business card from his wallet. "Call me. I think you're cute."

"You think I'm cute?" she laughed, "I'm anything but cute." She kept laughing after reading his card. "Pete Sheffield, Salesman, for Dave's Consumer Electronics? Oh my God, you're a cliché."

He smiled grudgingly.

She read the address. "And you work in a mall!" she screamed.

"Gonna call me?"

"Not likely, Mall Boy."

"You will, one day. Promise to keep the card?"

She shrugged. "Sure."

"Promise?"

"What, you want me to say it?"

"Yes. Promise me that it will accompany you on your descent into the Colorado River."

"Sure," she smiled, "I promise."

With a wave, he walked away, stopping at the street. "You never told me your name!"

"I know!" she said, waving back. Eventually, he gave up and continued down the sidewalk, without looking back this time. A knot formed in Deirdre's stomach. She was quite surprised later to discover that it wasn't gas. She actually missed him.

Another bus. Deirdre sits behind Cin and the brunette with the spaghetti straps, and plays with her lip piercing. She shrinks down and tries to be inconspicuous, something she's never been good at. The nervousness surprises her, though.

Inches from Deirdre's fingers, Cin's curls cascade down the seatback, dancing like marionettes whenever she moves her head. Deirdre gently touches them with the back of her hand. They feel like soft rain.

What the hell do I do now? The girls didn't notice when she followed them onto the bus and she hadn't considered anything past that. *Christ, I'm one of those Internet stalker psychos.*

The smudged words on the brunette's shoulder gives her an idea. Unzipping her knapsack, she removes her notebook and writes. When she's done, she rips out the page and hands it over the seat. "Here. Listen, sorry about this morning. I was cracked up on caffeine."

Cin stares suspiciously at Deirdre. "Do you go to Monroe?"

"No." She shakes the paper. "Take it. It's your poem." She nods at the other girl's shoulder. "Permanent ink my ass!"

Reluctantly, Cin accepts the page. "This is what I wrote?" she asks the brunette.

"I didn't read it," she answers and pivots her shoulder toward Cin. "You tell me."

Cin shakes her head. "Too smudged to read,"

"Wait," Deirdre says. "Why don't you know?"

"It was this morning," Cin says. "I barely remember last period." She hands the paper back.

"You don't want it?" Deirdre asks.

"What for?"

"What for? It's brilliant. You're amazing."

"Oh, it's just a Cin poem," the brunette says. "She writes them all the time. No big deal."

Cin pauses to consider this and her expression changes. She smiles at Deirdre, her eyes sparkling, and holds out her hand. "I'm Cin."

Deirdre's toes tingle as she closes her fingers around Cin's. They're so warm she almost melts.

"Number fifteen was on my fifteenth birthday," Deirdre says, adding sarcastically: "I was so clever. Thirteen on thirteenth would've probably been even cleverer, but I'd already missed the boat on that one. Is cleverer a word?"

They come to an intersection and wait for the walk signal. Deirdre sets her knapsack on the sidewalk.

"I think so, yes," Cin says.

Fifteen minutes has passed since the two of them got off the bus, leaving the rest of Cin's friends to continue on their way home. It seemed that once Cin discovered Deirdre was really interested in her poetry, she became interested in Deirdre. They are now on their way to Cin's house. Somehow their conversation immediately turned to talking about all the times Deirdre tried to kill herself, never once even coming close to success.

"Cool," Deirdre says. "So, Mom's across the street, visiting this woman who, I swear, looked just like a buzzard. She was a hundred and sixty or something. God only knows what they did over there. No doubt slamming shots of bourbon. Or maybe they smoked crack. Who knows?"

The light changes and Cin continues walking. Deirdre heaves her knapsack over her shoulder and catches up. "Anyway," she continues, out of breath, "She left her keys on the table. So, I run the garden hose from the tailpipe of her Turcell into the window and start the car."

"Which window?" Cin interrupts.

"Good question. To start, the driver's side. But the hose kept pulling out when I opened the door to get in. It was funny, really, in a pathetic way. I must have picked up that hose a dozen times before realizing it could go into the other window. On TV, they always use the driver's side, so I never considered anything else.

This is why TV is bad for the world. It's not the sex or violence, it's the dissemination of prepackaged ideas."

"Maybe they use longer hoses?" Cin suggests.

They stop at another light. Deirdre sets down her knapsack and wipes her sleeve across her face and tries to catch her breath. "So I get in, start the car, and close my eyes."

The light changes and Cin beats her to the knapsack. "I'd rather not see you die," she says.

Deirdre blushes. She can't remember ever blushing before and it annoys her that she is now. She covers with a laugh, so forced she instantly regrets it and stops. *Fuck, I can't just stop laughing; she'll think I'm a freak.* She laughs again, this time quieter, and slowly fades it out, hoping it sounds natural. Then she trips on her bootlace and tumbles onto the concrete.

Cin helps her up. "You okay?"

"Yeah." *Other than being a complete lunatic.* Her knees are scraped and bloody and her face an even deeper red than before. She follows Cin down a gravel road. "Where was I?"

"Hang on, check this out," Cin says. She takes Deirdre down a driveway to a small garden and squats beside a bunch of white flowers. "Aren't they beautiful?" Closing her eyes, Cin presses her face into a flower. "They're my favorites."

The tingle in Deirdre's feet begins to advance upwards. *Now they're beautiful,* she thinks. "What kind are they?"

"Orchids. You don't know orchids?"

"These orchids are splendid," Deirdre recites, "They spot and coil like snakes."

"Yes," Cin smiles, "*Sylvia* knew orchids. But *you* don't."

Deirdre is too amazed to blush. "You knew that was Sylvia Plath? From those two lines? That's unbelievable."

Cin gets up. "I went through a Sylvia phase. Anyway, tell me what *you* think of them? Most people say they look like vaginas."

Deirdre is unable to muster any sort of reply. After a nervous laugh, she starts back to the road.

Cin follows. "So, what were you thinking?"

Deirdre's mind races. "When? Just now? About the vag—"

"No, in the car where you were fifteen. You're still here, so something obviously stopped you."

"Oh, right." Deirdre clears her throat. "So, I'm sitting there, waiting to be asphyxiated, and I get the feeling something's missing. Then it hits me. The whole thing needs a soundtrack. So I go up to my room for a cassette tape."

"What tape?"

"Well, that's just it. I couldn't decide. I almost went for Brahms's *Lullaby*, but changed my mind. It seemed a bit contrived. I mean, if I was gonna do that, why not go for something ridiculous like 'Suicide Solution'? Remember that? Back before Ozzy went mental?"

"Didn't some kid actually commit suicide to that song?"

Deirdre frowns. "Yeah, that was another thing. Originality's important"

"So what did you decide on?"

" 'Helter Skelter.' "

Cin frowns. "Really?"

"Yeah, why?"

"I dunno. Didn't Manson do 'Helter Skelter' to death?"

"I was only fifteen, remember."

They stop at a fence. "This is my place," Cin says. She helps Deirdre over top and then follows, knapsack and all. "So, what went wrong?"

"I couldn't find the fucking tape. I looked everywhere. Know where it was?"

"Where?"

"In the car. I tore my entire room apart before I clued in. I ran back to the garage but it was too late."

"Your mom came home?"

"No, the car ran out of gas."

In the kitchen, Cin introduces her mom as Lexy and goes straight to the fridge. Lexy is standing on her head, something neither of them comment on.

"She's going to the Grand Canyon," Cin says.

"Ooh. Nice," Lexy says, still inverted.

" —to jump," Cin adds. She holds up a jug of orange juice to Deirdre. Deidre declines.

"Something you want to talk about, love?" Lexy asks Deirdre.

Cin answers for her. "No, she's good. She's put a lot of thought into it. It'll be her twenty-second try."

"Twenty-third," Deirdre corrects. She finds the ignoring of the headstanding quite disturbing, like when people pretend not to notice somebody's wheelchair.

"Are you just not very good at it?" Lexy asks.

"I'm a perfectionist," Deirdre says. "I think that's the problem."

"And why are you doing it?"

"Because the world sucks ass. It's way too depressing," Deirdre says. "Why are you on your head, anyway?"

Cin laughs and hands Deirdre a sandwich. "Now *that's* a question!" She leaves the room, motioning for Deirdre to follow.

"Will she be alive long enough to stay for dinner?" Lexy calls out.

"Yep," Cin answers. "And the night."

Deirdre studies the three empty picture frames hanging on Cin's wall wondering about the smashed glass.

"My art!" Cin explains.

"They're so sad."

"They are?" Cin looks disappointed. "They're supposed to echo spider webs. Could they be sad spider webs?"

Deirdre moves on to the bookcase, catching her reflection in the mirror on the way. "Oh my God, I look like a horror movie."

"You don't. You look good, considering you slept in a bus station. Wanna take a bath?"

"There must be quite a few things a hot bath won't cure, but I don't know many of them," she says. "It's Sylvia. From *The Bell Jar*."

"Yes, I know. You're a little obsessed with her, aren't you?"

Deirdre pulls the poetry book from her bag. "Yep. She even travels with me."

Cin flips through it. "Don't you find her a bit pretentious sometimes?" She reads the inscription written on the first page. "To DeeDee, love Mom. Who's DeeDee?"

"Me. Mom calls me DeeDee. I hate it. It's so girly."

"You're a girl."

"Yes, but I'm not four years old. Four-year-olds are called DeeDee. You're lucky. Your name's fucking cool."

Cin shrugs. "It doesn't bother me if people use my full name, though."

"Full name?" Deirdre asks.

Cin smiles. "Spell my name."

"S-I-N?"

"I knew it. You really do have your switch set firmly to macabre. It's C-I-N. Short for Cinderella."

"Not really?"

"Yep"

Deirdre thinks about it. "I think it's beautiful," she says. And she does.

"Well, I like DeeDee."

"Then you can call me DeeDee."

Cin hands the book back. "I just find Plath very depressing."

"Yeah, but I'm depressed, so it's all good. Besides, all good poetry is depressing. Well, almost."

"You believe that?" Cin asks. "Who do you classify as the best poet?"

After a pause, Deirdre says, "Shakespeare, maybe?"

"But you don't approve of his happy stuff?"

"Actually," Deirdre says, "I haven't read much Shakespeare."

Cin looks confused. "You just said—"

"I meant he's generally regarded as the best."

"DeeDee," Cin says, becoming serious. "You have some real issues, you know."

"Hello? Twenty-three attempted suicides? I know I have issues."

"Twenty-two. You haven't got to the canyon yet," Cin says. "But you really haven't made any *actual* attempts."

"What do you mean?"

"Death was never your intention. What does your mom think about all of them?"

"She doesn't know. Nobody does."

Cin blinks. "I don't understand. That's not even a cry for help. That's just . . . weird."

Deirdre shrugs. "Told you. I'm depressed."

"No you aren't," Cin says. She lifts her shirt. Her stomach is so scarred it looks like a roadmap.

Deirdre's eyes widen. "Oh my God! What happened?"

"I like to cut myself sometimes. Usually when I'm off my meds. They tell me it's clinical depression.

Anyway—" She pulls her shirt back down and stands up. "—it's bath time!"

The bathroom smells like a fairytale from the shelves full of oils, bath beads, bath balls, and bubble soap. Deirdre is thinking about her lonely shampoo bottle and bar of soap back home when Cin walks in without knocking and hands her a shirt. "Here. Wear this. I'll wash your clothes."

"Thanks," Deirdre says. She points to the shelves. "Big sale at the bath store?"

"Go nuts," Cin says. "Use whatever you want."

Deirdre waits for her to leave but she doesn't. "Oh, right, my clothes." She lifts her shirt an inch and hesitates.

"You want me to wait outside?"

Deirdre swallows. "No, this is fine." She undresses as quickly as possible, trying to stay in side profile so there's less to see. Twice she nearly trips while taking off her jeans. Cin leaves with the ball of clothes, shutting the door behind her. Deirdre is left staring at herself in the mirror hanging on its back. *Who the hell are you?*

After turning on the faucets, she feels like a witch tending to her cauldron, adding a pinch of this and a bit of that from nearly every product on the shelves. She doesn't stop until the tub's full. Bubbles fizz around her as she gets in, making her feel almost weightless.

She lies back. Closing her eyes, she imagines what it would be like to be a girlie girl, but her thoughts keep returning to Cin. She sinks deeper, feeling her whole body tingle. "Cinderella," she says quietly over and over. And each time it feels a little less strange.

The T-shirt Cin gave her is pink, covered in hearts, and hangs down to Deirdre's knees. She is wearing it when she returns to Cin's room and finds her on the computer. "What are you doing? Writing poetry?"

"No, chatting with my baby."

"Is he cute?" Deirdre asks, feeling very girlie girlish. "Invite him over!"

"*She* lives in Duluth. It's a bit of a walk."

"Ah," Deirdre says. "You like girls? Is *she* cute?"

"Hard to say yet. But that reminds me." She hands Deirdre a digital camera.

Deirdre plays with the buttons. When she looks back up, Cin is bent forward with her skirt and panties around her knees. "Take a picture!"

Butterflies swarming in Deirdre's stomach make their way to other places. "Of your ass?"

"Please."

Deirdre does and gives the camera back. Cin snaps a shot of Deirdre before connecting it to the computer.

"What are you doing now?"

"Sending the picture you took to whipNcream. She won't send hers until I do."

"whipNcream?"

"It's her online name, we haven't progressed to real ones yet. Okay, she's sending hers."

The printer hums to life and the picture creeps out the front. Deirdre grabs it. "What the fuck? The chick has a tumor or something."

Cin snatches it away. "It's a tattoo. My printer just sucks."

"A tattoo of what? A tumor?"

"No, a windmill." Cin goes over and closes her bedroom door. Taped to the back, a dozen similar pictures form a completed image of the most disturbing woman Deirdre has ever seen. The body parts are disproportionate, one breast hideously large, the head and legs ridiculously tiny. *If Picasso invented the camera, every photograph would look like this.*

"Her rear is going on the front of the door," Cin says. "We're starting with tushies. So, what do you think of her?"

"She's hideous."

Cin backs up and appraises. "Ya? Give her time, she grows on you."

"So you're—" Deirdre pauses. "—a lesbian?"

"I prefer Cervical Engineer. I take it you've never been with a girl?"

Feeling her face glow, Deirdre looks down. Her fingers touch her piercing.

"You're *not* a complete virgin? Don't tease me."

Deirdre looks everywhere but at Cin.

"You are! You really are!"

Glancing at the computer screen, Deidre gets an opportunity to change the subject. "whipNcream sent you a message. You should answer it."

Cin goes over and shuts it off. "No, it's too late," she says, with a wicked grin. "I think it's bedtime."

When Deirdre wakes, the room is cast in the morning sun, and her cheek is bathing in a puddle of drool. She is alone. Rubbing her eyes, she thinks about last night and laughs. *I told her I loved her. I love Cinderella.* Pulling on her shirt, she follows the glorious smell of coffee to the kitchen.

Lexy is sitting on the counter, right way up. "I was just coming to wake you," she says. "Coffee?"

"God yes. Where's Cin?"

"School." Lexy points to a bag sitting on the table. "She left you that."

It is covered in sparkles and shimmering. A pink heart tied to one of the handles says, "To DeeDee. Luv Cinderella." Two days ago, Deirdre would have wretched at the sight of it. This morning, she barely contains a squeal.

Inside is a picture of Deirdre framed in smashed glass with a note taped to the front.

> Dee,
>
> The happy poems might be better hiders, but you can find them anywhere. You just have to know what to look for. I think you'll have a better idea now.
>
> Your friend,
> Cinderella
> PS. Don't confuse love with feeling good.
> PPS. Go back to your natural hair color.

I told Cin I'd drive you home to Vancouver," Lexy says, "or halfway to Arizona. Your choice."

Deirdre smiles. "Let's make it home. I'm actually terrified of heights anyway."

She spends the trip quietly spinning Pete's business card in her fingers, wondering if he likes blondes.

My Lame Summer Journal by Brandon Harris Grade 7 *won the Surrey International Writers' Conference Storyteller's award in 2004. This story won it in 2005.*

But Not Forgotten *came out of another workshop. The requirements were that the story had to feature the chocolate shop down the hill from where us writers were being sequestered for two weeks.*

I couldn't think of anything. However, the house we were in was stockpiled with unimaginable collections and my room was crammed with stuffed bears. Since I wasn't writing, I decided to count them.

Number seventy-one was painting a picture. Ninety-six turned out to be two elderly bears sipping tea. My brain combined these into one and voila!

It's true. Ideas are everywhere. And sometimes they even show up in boxes on your doorstep postmarked from Wichita.

But Not Forgotten

"Moving, with a sweet twist of an ending."
- Diana Gabaldon, New York Times Bestseller

"A wonderful story, beautifully executed. The isolation of old age is there, and so is the invisibility and facelessness of old age in the eyes of youth. Charlie, the protagonist, is a wonderful and convincing character."
- Jack Whyte, International Bestseller

October 5
Pick up package,
noon today—Greyhound

Charlie no longer trusts his thoughts so he writes them down. The trick allows him to hide his fading mind from his children so they won't move him out of his place into some sort of home for senior citizens. According to his notebooks, he's been keeping it up for fifteen months.

He is in his bedroom, sitting at the metal card table. He found the table at a garage sale on Willow Street a month ago. It cost him ten dollars, eight for the table and two more that he gave to Danny Winfield, the neighbor boy, to carry it home for him.

Charlie's bed is unmade. He rarely makes it anymore. Right now, he can't remember where it came from, but he's had it since he moved in here six years ago. The room is dark. He likes it dark and keeps the thick drapes over the windows tightly closed. There is a brass desk lamp on the table that he uses to light the room. He's had it for twenty years. He and his wife, Ilsa, brought the lamp back with them from England in 1974, a vacation he remembers well.

The notebook on the table catches his attention.

Pick up package,
noon today—Greyhound

A package is sitting for him at the bus station. He's been waiting for it for a long time, and still hasn't arranged a ride to run and get it. The phone his son Greg gave him for his birthday last year is on the table beside the lamp. He remembers opening the gift on his eighty-fourth birthday. Greg and his family flew all the way from Boston special just for it, and Charlie finally got to see his granddaughters. Beautiful girls.

No, he reminds himself, they are women now. The oldest named Felicia and the other —

He can't remember. And now that he thinks about it, it wasn't this past birthday, but his eightieth that Greg came out for. Four years ago. The older you get, the more elusive time and memories become. He tries to recall the name of his son's wife but can't. Has he really had the phone for four years? Why is he thinking about the phone?

His package. He presses the button on the receiver that dials his daughter Kelly's telephone number. Kelly only lives forty-five minutes away in Tacoma and she usually stops in at least once a week to make sure he's doing okay. She's starting to notice something is wrong, he thinks. Greg used to call a couple times a week but lately it's been more like once or twice a month. Charlie's pretty sure Greg just moved to a new company so he's probably been busy.

"Hello?" Kelly answers.

"Hi Kelly, it's Dad."

"Dad? Is everything okay?"

"Everything is fine," Charlie says. Picking the pen up from beside his notebook, he taps it twice on the page. "I was wondering if you were planning on coming over today."

"No Dad, not today. Today is Tuesday, I have to work today. I'm working afternoons now, remember?"

Charlie writes this down.

Kelly works afternoons now

"How is Frank doing?" he asks. "I haven't seen him in a while."

A pause and Kelly says, "Dad, Frank and I split up two years ago."

Charlie sighs and writes this in his notebook too. "I'm sorry, honey," he says. "Slipped my mind. Can you believe it?"

"Are you sure you're okay, Dad?"

"Yes, I'm fine. I'm calling because I need a ride to the bus station. The Greyhound."

"What do you mean? Why do you need to go to the bus station?" He hears the concern in her voice and wishes he hadn't called. He hates making her worry.

"Dad," she asks, "would you like me to call Doctor Kent?"

"No, Kelly, I'm fine. Really. I have a package I need to pick up at the Greyhound."

"What kind of package?" she asks. "Who sent you a package?" He still hears the worry.

"It's—" he hesitates because he's never told anyone before. Why does it feel like he shouldn't? Why does it feel like a secret? There's no rational reason not to tell her the truth, so he does. "It's chocolates, Kelly."

"Chocolates?" he hears a slight laugh in her voice. "Dad, you can't eat chocolate, you have diabetes. Who would send you a box of chocolates on a bus? Chocolate could *kill* you. I think I should call your doctor."

"No," he says, a little too gruff. It immediately quiets his tone. "No, Kelly, really, I'm fine. I'm sorry to have bothered you."

"You're *sure* you're fine?"

"Yes, honey, I'll see you on the weekend."

She pauses and then, "Okay. But I'm going to call later and check on you, all right?"

"That'll be fine," he says. "Goodbye."

He sets the telephone back in its cradle and drums his fingers on the top trying to figure out how to get to the Greyhound. He flips to the back of the notebook where he has photographs of friends and family with notes beneath the pictures.

Evelyn. His son's wife is named Evelyn. And his youngest daughter is Chelsea. Why couldn't he remember that? Anyway, he can't call any of them for a ride because they live in Boston.

He decides he'll take a city bus and just go on his own. The Greyhound is only five miles away, just this side of downtown.

He thinks there's a bus stop just a block up Chestnut, the street he lives on. He's pretty sure he and Danny Winfield, the neighbor boy, passed it when they brought the card table home from the garage sale on Willow. Any downtown bus must go right past the Greyhound. Turning to a fresh page in his notebook he writes:

Bus to Greyhound for package

Then he writes:

663 Chestnut

It would be embarrassing to forget his address. He can't imagine it ever happening, but why take chances? Carefully, he tears the page out and folds it once in half and carries it through his kitchen and into his living room where he sets it on top of his recliner while he puts on his coat and shoes. In here, only a gossamer curtain hangs over the picture window behind his old sofa. It's a grey, overcast day. A hat day. But Charlie's hat isn't on its usual peg.

It's not on the oak coffee table where he sometimes finds it, or even on top of the television. He checks the top of the two cherry knickknack display cases he bought Ilsa for Christmas of 1988 so she would have a place to display her Swarovski crystal collection. Oh how she smiled when he gave her those. "You spent too much. You don't have to always go all out. Oh quit looking so smug about it. You're such a little kid sometimes. Yes, of course I love them." So much she cried.

God he misses her.

Two paintings of her hang on the other side of the room. She's young in them, twenty-six—he thinks—in the one on the right, and twenty-eight in the one on the left where she's holding Greg. He painted them back when he used to paint. They aren't very good (he was never a great painter) but, to Ilsa, they certainly seemed to be. So much so that when he moved into his new place six years ago, he brought them with. There were plenty of others he didn't bother bringing, but these two he felt compelled to. Because these two had been her favorites.

Of all the rooms in the house, this one's the hardest to be in because it's the one that isn't his. It's theirs. The paintings, the sofa, the coffee table, even the television. These things belonged to them, not like the card table in the bedroom. Not like his bed. Those are his. They aren't filled with memories pushing him away.

Charlie collects himself, looks through the gossamer at the misty day outside.

His hat. He was looking for his hat.

It's on the kitchen table. He remembers now. He sets the hat on his head, takes his paper of little reminders, and leaves his house, carefully locking the door behind him. With a deep breath, he cleanses his lungs with cold October air. Winter was always Ilsa's favorite season, but Charlie's is fall. Fall is the changing of the guard— those last few brush strokes when you discover how the painting is going to turn out. Things end. They die out. But, to Charlie anyway, in those last couple months of life they are at their most beautiful.

He is right about the bus stop; it's just a block up Chestnut. Holding his reminder paper, he sits on the wooden bench and waits.

Across the street, a blue jay lands on a brown picket fence running roadside of a field. Charlie used to watch birds a lot more when Ilsa was still here. From the beginning of their marriage until she died, they'd go for long walks almost every night and take in nature. He would talk about becoming an artist, she would go on about one day being a poet. Neither of them was good enough to do either professionally, but they didn't care. That's why they call them dreams.

Funny, but when he looks back at that time now, that is the dream. To go back and walk with her one more time. To have her grab his arm and stop him, whispering *Look!* and pointing out a squirrel. Back then, his dreams were in the future, and now his dreams are in the past. It seems there should have been a point along the way when the two passed each other and the dreams and now were the same, but he can't remember one.

"Hey, are you waiting for this bus?" asks a man in a uniform standing beside Charlie. He's the driver of the bus stopped on the road in front of him.

Charlie is about to say no, he isn't, when he glances down at the paper in his hands. He unfolds it and re-members. The driver tells him that yes, this bus goes right to the Greyhound.

Charlie takes the seat behind the driver, the one re-served for elderly people. The black woman sitting across from him stares straight ahead out the front win-dow of the bus, but her two children stare at Charlie. The girl is youngest. Charlie guesses maybe three, but he's never been very good with such things. Her hair is braided with pink and yellow butterflies and she's wearing a yellow dress. She seems scared of him and huddles close to her mom. The boy is seven or eight, he's wearing a light blue dress shirt, slacks, and sneakers.

"You two look very nice," Charlie says.

The boy continues to stare, ignoring the comment completely. The girl reaches around her mom's waist and buries her head into her sweater. The woman ignores everything except the view out the front window.

Charlie thinks about Greg and his family out in Boston. They moved back east in 1979 and Charlie has only seen his son four times since then. In 1980 right after the wedding, and in 1981 just after Greg's wife became pregnant with Felicia. He can't remember Greg's wife's name. The third time, Greg came back alone for Ilsa's funeral in 1998. He only met his two granddaughters at his eightieth—

"Sir, this is the Greyhound bus station," the driver calls back to Charlie.

"Thank you," Charlie says and walks down the steps onto the sidewalk. The wind has picked up, blowing bits of trash past his feet. He walks inside and checks with the young man at the information kiosk who points him in the direction of PARCEL PICKUP.

Charlie is third in line.

A man with long hair and a short beard gets in line behind him. A young girl with him has black hair and an earring in her nose. She is chewing bubble gum, and her hair and makeup are very black—except her lips which are bright red, reminding Charlie somehow of Christmas. He guesses she is fourteen, but he's not good at such things. The man must notice Charlie looking at her because he laughs and says, "Kids today. What are you going to do, huh?"

Charlie smiles. "I think she looks nice." He doesn't really, but he likes making children feel good. She acts like she doesn't even hear him, looking over at some boys standing by the pop machine.

"I dunno about that," the man says. "Do you have kids?"

"Yes," Charlie says. "I have two. My boy's name is Greg and my girl's name is Kelly." The girl in the black make-up with the bright red lips blows a bubble and finally looks at Charlie. Charlie says, "She's probably not much older than you. She's—" and he pauses because he's suddenly confused. He remembers Kelly being fourteen, but he also remembers Kelly graduating from high school. He remembers Kelly going to law school for two years and then dropping out and taking a job as a bookkeeper. He shakes his head, "Sorry, that's not what I meant. She's considerably older than you . . . "

But the man and his daughter are no longer listening, and the person behind the parcel pickup window is calling for Charlie to come over. He does. He shows the man his identification and the man presents him with his package—a cardboard box sealed with packing tape. It's about a foot and a half long by a foot high and a foot deep. Even though he knows exactly what it is and where it came from, Charlie double checks the manifest:

ROCKY MOUNTAIN CHOCOLATE FACTORY
3500 SOUTH HIGHWAY 101
LINCOLN CITY, OR

Charlie is still holding his little reminder sheet. He folds it a second time and puts it in the pocket of his coat before collecting his box and carrying it back out to the street. He crosses at the light, just in time to catch the bus heading back home. He tells the driver his address before taking his seat.

The package sits on his lap all the way home and Charlie thinks of Ilsa. He remembers the day they met on a beach in Lincoln City, Oregon. It was 1954. The first thing he noticed were her eyes. Chocolate brown. And her lips. They looked so soft. And when she smiled, her cheeks dimpled in a way that made Charlie's stomach flip. And when she laughed, her head tilted back and her blonde curls shook down her back and Charlie fell so deeply in love he knew he would never get back out again.

And he never did.

He lived in Lincoln City; she was only there on holidays. An hour later he took her to a little chocolate shop up on the highway. He can't remember the name now, but he hasn't been able to for a long time. It was their first date. They spent every day of the next week together, and then she went back to San Francisco. He called her every night and drove down almost every weekend. Six months later, they were engaged. Six months after that, they married and moved into a small house together just outside of San Francisco.

Ilsa was a hopeless romantic and Charlie loved it. She cherished everything about their relationship, especially things like first dates, and insisted on going back to the chocolate shop once a year for their anniversary. They kept the tradition up until Greg was born, and then life got in the way for a while; Charlie worked hard for a string of job promotions and Ilsa stayed at home and had babies.

But just for a while.

In 1970, Charlie's work moved them to Seattle. The kids were older, and Charlie and Ilsa started getting back to being lovers. And they were still very much in love. That year for their anniversary, Ilsa suggested they drive down the coast and stop again at the chocolate shop.

Only it was gone. It was now an antique store. Charlie could tell Ilsa was disappointed. It made him sad.

Then, twenty years later, in 1990, Charlie drove down the coast to stay with an old friend in Newport who had just lost his wife to cancer. He drove through Lincoln City, slowing when he got to the stretch of road that brought back so many memories of his courtship to Ilsa. He looked for the old chocolate shop that was now an antique store. Only, it was no longer an antique store.

It was a chocolate shop again. The Rocky Mountain Chocolate Factory.

When their anniversary came around that year, Charlie surprised Ilsa by taking her back to the place she thought no longer existed. And it wasn't really the same place, but, in a way, it was. And that was close enough.

After that, they went every year until Ilsa had her stroke, July of 1998.

The bus pulls to the curb and the driver tells Charlie it's his stop. Charlie carries the package off of the bus.

The day has grown darker and the clouds look like pregnant guppies ready to burst at any time. The walk home is brisk, and Charlie can feel a light sweat on his face when he finally arrives.

He sets the package down on his front porch to unlock the door. Occasional drops of rain splatter onto his head, his arms, his hand. "Made it back just in time," Ilsa would've said.

Inside, Charlie hangs his hat on its peg and his coat on the one beside it. Then he takes off his shoes before going back out for the package on the porch. He carries it through the living room and kitchen, then down the narrow passage of creaky stairs leading to the basement, flicking the light switch along the way.

It's been almost a year since he came down last, and the air still has a sweetness to it that makes him smile. His easel, his brushes, his wooden stool, everything's all where he left it. On the other side of the room is a small kitchen. A dozen pots and saucepans are stacked neatly beneath a deep laundry sink. He sets the package on the short countertop between the sink and the old gas stove.

Five paintings of Ilsa hang around the room. They aren't great, but Ilsa would have loved them, and that makes Charlie smile even more. *Why do you go to such trouble? You waste too much time thinking about me. Oh quit looking so smug about it. You're such a little kid sometimes. Yes, of course I love them.* He wipes his eyes with his sleeve.

Using one of his keys, he cuts the package open revealing the gold box inside with the Rocky Mountain Chocolate Factory logo printed on the top. An envelope with Charlie's name handwritten on the front contains a letter:

> My Darling Charlie,
>   Although we are apart
>   you are always in my heart
>   I may be gone
>   but you are not forgotten
>   I will love you throughout eternity.
>   Happy anniversary, my love,
> Forever Yours, Ilsa

He reads the note three times before pinning it up beside the other five. Each one different, and each written in his wife's beautiful hand. He doesn't know when she made the arrangements for the deliveries, or for how many years they will come, but it's the most thoughtful gift anyone could give. Like a child waiting for Christmas morning, Charlie waits all year with growing anticipation and hope for another love letter from beyond the grave.

Walking to the stove, he lights the four top burners, and pulls pots and saucepans clanging and banging from under the sink, sorting them in rows on the countertop. He takes the box of chocolates from the package and opens it.

Using the guide sheet packaged inside, he begins sorting the contents into different pots. For some, like the chocolate cherry bombs, the peanut butter balls, and the caramel truffle, he cuts them in half with a knife and, using a spoon, scoops the fillings into one pot and puts the shells into another.

He puts the first four onto the burners. While they melt into a liquid, he places a new canvas on his easel and sorts through his brushes. The room is bathed in an intoxicating—almost sexual—aroma, making Charlie swoon. When the chocolate is ready, he spreads the four colors onto his palette and takes them to the canvas.

Using his number eight brush, he mixes some peppermint bark into the white chocolate and adds just a pinch of pecan. Then, with a clean graceful stroke, he starts to work on his sixth painting since the death of his wife.

And as always it begins with the outline of a face.

A face he will never forget.

The face of an angel.

The Author

Michael Hiebert is an award-winning author of novels and short stories. His latest book *Dream With Little Angels* is being released by Kensington Publishing Corp. in New York.

Michael lives in the Lower Mainland of British Columbia, Canada where it is cold and wet in the winter and warm (and sometimes *still* wet) in the summer. There are cougars, and bears, and deer. He has a dog named Chloe, three children, and enough books that it became no fun to move quite a long time ago.

He enjoys crafting surprising stories that cross genres. He's been writing most of his life, but really has spent the past decade perfecting his craft. His writing has been described as a blend of the mysterious and the fantastic. He likes to find the redemption in the horrific, the surviving heart still beating among all the sorrow, the beauty lost somewhere in all the ugliness of the world.

You can follow Michael on his website at **www.michaelhiebert.com**. From there, you can link to him on Facebook, Twitter, read his blog, and do all sorts of other things. There's even a free audio book to download! Make sure you sign up for his newsletter to receive exciting news on new releases, and get discounts on his books.

You can also leave Michael a message, post a comment on his blog, or send him any sort of information you think he might be interested in. Human heads are not something he's interested in. Just wanted to point that out.

If you enjoyed this book (or even if you didn't), why not review it on Amazon.com, Barnes & Noble, or anywhere else on the web you can find to post a review? If you do, be sure to drop Michael a note telling him about it so he can check it out.

He looks forward to hearing from you!

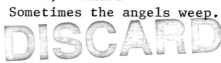